BITTER TEARS

WAR GIRL SERIES, BOOK 7

MARION KUMMEROW

CONTENTS

Reader Group   v

Chapter 1   1
Chapter 2   9
Chapter 3   19
Chapter 4   27
Chapter 5   34
Chapter 6   44
Chapter 7   53
Chapter 8   59
Chapter 9   66
Chapter 10   71
Chapter 11   78
Chapter 12   87
Chapter 13   92
Chapter 14   98
Chapter 15   108
Chapter 16   115
Chapter 17   123
Chapter 18   132
Chapter 19   140
Chapter 20   146
Chapter 21   154
Chapter 22   158
Chapter 23   164
Chapter 24   171
Chapter 25   178
Chapter 26   191
Chapter 27   198
Chapter 28   207
Chapter 29   214
Chapter 30   220

Author's Notes 231
Also by Marion Kummerow 235
Contact Me 237

READER GROUP

Marion's Reader Group

Sign up for my reader group to receive exclusive background information and be the first one to know when a new book is released.

http://kummerow.info/subscribe

CHAPTER 1

April 1945, Poland

Artillery shells exploded. Shouts, both in Russian and in German, echoed in the eerie silence between explosions.

Katrina Zdanek huddled inside the small farmhouse, trying in vain to chase away the fear. She longed for a time when life wasn't so violent or scary. The fighting between the Red Army and the German Wehrmacht had been getting more intense over the last few weeks. At the normally quiet and peaceful lake only a stone's throw from the farm, both armies had reached an impasse after their sluggish efforts to overtake one another locked them into a stalemate.

Mrs. Jaworski huddled beside her, breathing heavily and pressing a rosary to her heart, the beads moving between her fingers as she recited *Hail Marys* uncountable times.

Katrina looked at the older woman, who'd kindly sheltered her and Richard, her boyfriend, on her farm after the Nazis had burnt down the Zdanek farm. "Don't you think we should leave this place?" Katrina asked for the umpteenth time.

"Never. I was born on this soil and I will die on it," Mrs. Jaworski stubbornly replied.

Die you will, if we don't get out of the line of fire, Katrina murmured to herself. Since the front line had reached their village weeks ago, the world around them had become a living hell. Far from the quick liberation everyone had hoped for, they'd been stuck in a perpetual battleground like innocent prisoners caught in the crossfire of a futile war. The opposing armies were fighting tooth and nail for the strategic advantage of having the protection of the lake on their side.

With the world erupting in flames, most everyone had abandoned their homes and fled to less embattled areas.

A shell exploded outside, the reverberations shaking Katrina's bones. She ducked her head even deeper, trying to become one with the stone wall that protected her body from the deadly impact. Half a minute later, the smoke from the explosion wafted through the shattered window and made her gag.

Her heart constricted with fear over Richard's safety. Her boyfriend, a German Wehrmacht deserter, had been out at night, foraging the woods for something to eat. Now, heavily under attack, she worried not only for her own life, but also for his. *Where on earth is he? Please, God... let him be alive and unharmed.* Although he'd shed his uniform almost a year ago and taken on a fake identity as a Polish civilian, he was still in constant danger of being shot on the spot by either the Germans or the Russians should his real identity be revealed.

During a lull in the fighting, she held her breath, listening intently. An eerie silence cloaked her surroundings until she heard the telltale cuckoo call, and a burden fell from her shoulders.

Richard was alive!

Moments later the skirmish continued in full force and Katrina pressed her bony back against the wall, holding her hands over her ears and closing her eyes.

Hours passed and finally the battle noises subsided. Katrina dared to peer out the window, the picture of utter destruction grabbing her heart with an icy hand. She'd lost her own home... watched it burn to the ground, unable to do anything as the Nazis had rejoiced in adding fuel to the fire.

For the past eight months she and Richard had found a second home with Mrs. Jaworski, the mother of a dear friend. Katrina wondered what had become of her friend, Bartosz. He had fought alongside her brothers, Stan and Jarek, with the Polish partisans. Almost a year ago the Nazi pigs had tortured Jarek to death, leaving herself and his twin Stan with an empty space in their hearts.

Stan and Bartosz had stayed with the partisans, and none of them had the time to mourn a brother and a good friend. Not during this god-awful war, not when people were dying like flies all round. Her heart grew heavy and she willed the thoughts away. Now wasn't the time to dwell upon grief. No, now was the time to fight for survival.

She got up and shook the dust from her skirt and blouse,

before she held out a hand to help up Mrs. Jaworski. She had to give the old woman credit. Despite being pale as a ghost and shaking like aspen leaves, she resumed her tasks without uttering a complaint and started to sweep the floor.

Minutes later, Richard strolled into the house, his blond hair tousled, his beard badly shaved and his clothes covered in mud and thistle, but a huge grin softened his expression. God, how she loved this man who never stopped looking at the bright side of life. Despite having served two winters on the Eastern Front, deep in the Russian tundra, he refused to succumb to the dire straits of war, and somehow found a reason to flash his adorable boyish smile every day.

"Look what I found," he said, and held up a bloodied, half torn-apart rabbit. The poor thing must have been hit. But now it would give them a delicious, hearty meal. Food had been scarce since the front line had reached their area and they were running low on everything except water.

"Goodness." Katrina stepped forward to take the rabbit and pressed a kiss on Richard's rough lips. She didn't tell him how worried she'd been and she didn't say a word about how bad today had been at the house. Some things were better left unsaid.

"It looks like both armies have entrenched themselves, waiting for reinforcements. It's only gonna get worse and we should get out of here while we're still alive," he said, holding Katrina by her shoulders.

"I'm not going anywhere," Mrs. Jaworski said. "If I leave now, what will there be to return to once the war ends? Nothing, I tell you. I won't have my farm and no place to live." She took the rabbit from Katrina's hand and skinned it.

"I'll get water from the lake." Katrina grabbed two buckets on a stick that she placed across her shoulders.

"Let me help you." Richard picked up a pail and hurried to follow her.

They walked the half a mile down to the lake in silence, before Richard finally said, "We need to convince her to leave, or we'll all die."

"I know," Katrina said. They'd had this conversation countless times. "But we can't leave her here by herself. She's been so kind all these months."

Richard nodded. "She's persisting in the hopes at least one of her three sons will return and find her at the farm." His voice became dreary.

Katrina squeezed his hand. Without saying a word, she understood his feelings. After deserting the Wehrmacht a year ago he hadn't heard from his family and had no idea whether they were still alive or not.

"The uncertainty is bad," she said. She hadn't heard anything from her own brother, Stan, for months. And she'd all but given up hope of seeing her oldest brother, Piotr, ever again. He'd been missing since Hitler's invasion in 1939.

"It is."

They washed at the lake, accompanied by incessant battle noises. Then they filled their buckets, before Richard wrapped his arms around her and said, "Relax. It'll all be over soon."

"Let's hope so," she answered, pressing her body against his thin but muscular one. In his arms she always felt protected, and soon enough, his nearness dissolved the tension in her body and she sagged against him.

"That's better." He gave her a long, passionate kiss on her lips, before he broke away. "We better get going. I don't like leaving Mrs. Jaworski alone for long."

"Me, neither."

~

Walking half a mile with two heavy buckets full of water was strenuous, and Katrina sighed with relief when the farmhouse came into sight. But the next moment she stopped in her tracks and Richard bumped into her from behind, spilling some of the precious water.

"What's up?" he asked, as a tremble rocketed through her body. The stone building lay in wreckage, columns of smoke rising into the otherwise blue sky. She set down her pails, ready to sprint to the house, but Richard put a heavy hand on her shoulder. "Don't."

"We have to go look for her."

"First, we must wait until the soldiers are gone," he said, tightening his grip.

She defied the urge to fight him because she knew he was right. A rash action would only bring harm . If she barged into the farm right now, it might be a suicide mission. "You can stop holding me, I won't run off." She turned her head and smiled.

"Let me go ahead first."

From experience she knew it wouldn't help to argue with him, so she nodded. Richard ducked into the high grass and snuck up on the farmhouse. After several minutes he stood and waved her forward.

Leaving the pails of water behind, she hurried over to where he waited.

"All gone. We can have a look."

But as soon as they entered the yard, Katrina put a hand across her mouth at the ghastly sight of Mrs. Jaworski torn to shreds. Searching for Richard's gaze, she noticed the tightening of his jaw, a sure sign of his hapless anger. "We'll bury her and then we leave."

Katrina nodded and put her feet into motion toward the ruins of the house, to see if there was anything she could salvage. She didn't find much. Some pieces of cutlery. Metal crockery. A big shawl. A book that had miraculously survived. She rubbed the dirt from the copy of *Wilhelm Tell* by Friedrich Schiller and wondered if the book served as an omen for their own lives. Shuddering, she knotted the shawl into a backpack and filled it with everything useful she found, including some stray potatoes lying in the yard.

Meanwhile, Richard dug a grave for Mrs. Jaworski in her yard and was about to lower her inside when Katrina returned. With wet eyes she watched the kind woman slip into the dark earth, and she folded the dead woman's hands in prayer, before she helped him fill up the grave.

"I liked her, too," Richard said as he took Katrina's hand.

To prevent herself from tearing up, she showed him the backpack and said, "I gathered everything useful I could find. Including a copy of *Wilhelm Tell.*"

"How fitting. Let's go." Richard's lip quivered slightly, revealing the depth of his own emotion. A little shiver of grief and regret tugged at Katrina's heart. But now was not the time to mourn.

"But where will we go?" The Polish Home Army partisans they had been providing with food came to her mind, but the partisan unit had left the area weeks ago to join fighting units elsewhere.

"I don't know."

Sounds of artillery in the distance heightened her sense of urgency and she looked into Richard's eyes. "The woods."

CHAPTER 2

Two days had passed since their flight from the farm, and the savage fighting raged on. The forest wasn't a great place to live, although it was safer than the ravaged villages. Richard held Katrina close, shivering in his damp clothes. As much as nature needed the life-giving moisture, he sure could do without the constant drizzle raining down on them.

Katrina moved in his arms and opened her eyes, looking at him. "What has you so worried?"

"Hmm …let's see." He tried a crooked grin. "Right now, I can't think of anything to worry about."

As he had intended, she laughed out loud and snuggled tighter into his arms. As long as they had each other, he'd never lose faith in a better future. His stomach growled, reminding him they hadn't eating anything remotely filling for the last two days.

"We could see whether we can return to the village," Katrina suggested.

It wasn't a good idea, actually it was an *awful* idea, but there wasn't much else they could do. If they hid out in the forest with the constant rain and cold and without food or shelter, they wouldn't last much longer.

"I think it's a great idea," he said after a slight pause.

"You hate it."

"I do, but since there's nothing else…" He didn't bother to finish his sentence.

When they arrived at the edge of the hill overlooking the village with Mrs. Jaworski's farm, only rubble greeted them. Piles of stones strewn across the landscape. Scorched earth where fields had lain. Only the big green lake looked as still and peaceful as ever.

"What now?" Katrina tried to sound brave, but he knew her too well to miss the unshed tears in her voice.

"We can't stay here."

"I know. I've been thinking… I have extended family near Breslau – a cousin of my mother," Katrina said.

"Breslau? That's in Germany."

"Not anymore."

"What does this mean?" Richard stared at Katrina. These days accurate information was hard to come by, and without a radio at the farm they had been confined to the irregular newspaper and gossip in the village.

"About a month ago the state national council, Krajowa Rada Narodowa, with the backing of Stalin, announced that all German possessions east of the Oder-Neisse Line have been vacated and abandoned. Two weeks later they announced the foundation of the voivodeships Upper Silesia, Lower Silesia and a few more."

Richard balled his hands into fists. How dare the

communist puppets tell those lies and annex big parts of Germany? "You never told me."

"I must have forgotten."

A shudder ripped through him at the magnitude of that lie. He cocked his head, grinding his teeth. "And the real reason?"

She gave a little sigh. "I knew you'd have a fit of rage and would mope around for days. Look, I don't like what's happening either, but there's nothing we can do. And I don't have to remind you that it was your country that started this war."

"Hmm." He stubbornly stared into the distance for a while, then said, "I'm not going there."

"Why not?"

"Because... it's too dangerous." His personal feelings aside, there was no real reason why he resisted her suggestion. They couldn't keep hiding out in the woods, and one place was as good as the next one.

"It's in fact much safer with my relatives than on our own."

As much as he hated to admit it, she was right. Having the protection of friendly locals would help him to remain undiscovered. Mrs. Jaworski had known his true identity, and had dodged the nosy questions of the other villagers by introducing him as a distant, and grumpy, cousin from up North. He'd never ventured into the village and never talked to anyone.

But arriving as newcomers in another village would pique the curiosity of people and they'd ask all kinds of questions. Once they did, he'd be found out in no time at all, despite his passable Polish skills and forged papers.

"Are you sure we can stay with them?"

"If they are still alive, yes. If they aren't, we can seek a place to live in Breslau itself. Your chances to blend in are much better in a big city."

Again, she was right. "Hmm. Maybe. But it's too far away."

"It's not that far, about seventy miles southwest."

"And how do you suggest we get there? Call a taxi?"

Katrina laughed out loud. "I would like to do that, but I doubt there's a single taxi left within a thousand miles."

"See, it's impossible!" he insisted, his stomach churning at the idea of living in a place that had been German for so long and now suddenly belonged to another nation. He didn't want to see all the German citizens who, no doubt, would now be harassed in one form or another by the new Polish government.

"It's not impossible and you're being stubborn. Do you have a better idea?"

Richard scratched his beard while he pondered it, but nothing sprang to mind. Hiding out in the woods would only draw suspicion to him when they'd inevitably be found by the new occupying army. And the Russians didn't take fondly to Wehrmacht soldiers trying to evade captivity.

If he wanted to stick to his disguise as a Polish farmer, he had to do what a Pole would do. He had to go and live with Katrina's relatives, even if they lived in the heartland of German cultural heritage.

"Alright, you win. Let's start walking. We have quite a journey ahead of us."

It might end up being a crazy undertaking, destined to fail, but it was the only viable option they had. They walked for endless hours, and with each step, his hunger increased. Suddenly Katrina stopped and bent down to pick a green stalk.

"What's that?" he asked, eying the plant suspiciously. He'd still not gotten used to her feeding him with whatever edible thing she found on the path.

"Water mint. Chew it carefully and the oil will help suppress the hunger," she said, picking a few leaves from the stem and holding them out to him.

Instinctively he backed away, unsure whether he wanted to put the leaves in his mouth. "Are you sure this isn't poisonous?"

"Richard," she laughed out loud. "I learned the subject of herbs and medicine from my parents, who were healers. And water mint is one of the stock plants of herbal medicine. We used to have it in the garden on our farm. So, yes, I'm sure it's not poisonous."

With defiance in his gaze he took the leaves and shoved them into his mouth.

"Don't swallow them. You have to chew several minutes to free up the oil. Normally, I would crush it finely in a mortar or use boiling water to make an infusion, but since we're short on kitchen gear, our teeth will have to do the work," she said, laughing.

The water mint tasted surprisingly good and after a while the fresh, tangy aroma fooled him into thinking his stomach was full. When night broke, they found a forlorn hut with an intact fireplace. Gathering up wood from the surroundings they made a fire and settled on the floor in front of it.

Katrina poured the last water from her bottle into the

only pot they'd rescued from the destroyed farmhouse and heated it on the fire, putting several leaves inside.

"I'd rather not ask what this is," Richard teased her when she handed him a cup of the liquid.

"Tea."

It tasted slightly bitter, but mostly it was hot and warmed his tired bones from the inside. Minutes after drinking their tea, they both fell into an exhausted sleep. Right before drifting off, he thought about finding real food lest they end up starving to death.

The next morning he woke with the dawn, cold, stiff and sore. Katrina was cuddled into his arms, her small body pressed against his, sharing his warmth. They'd untied the shawl-backpack and used it as a blanket, but it hadn't been nearly enough to keep out the chills of early spring.

He was reminded of his days fighting at the Eastern Front, deep in the Russian tundra. Some nights they'd frozen to the ground in the trenches and many a day he'd joked with his comrades that his entire being would melt into a puddle should the harsh winter ever cease – and should he still be alive.

Two years later and he was still here. Most of his comrades hadn't shared the same fate. Those who hadn't fallen had been marched away into Russian captivity and Karl… his best friend… had died on him just before Katrina had given him a second chance at life.

Richard brushed a strand of hair from her face. He'd been captivated by her warrior spirit from the first moment he'd seen her, during the raid in Baluty, fighting him like a lioness. She hadn't known he wanted to help, had assumed the worst.

Katrina moved in his arms and his heart flowed over with love. He owed her everything. Weeks after that incident, she'd saved him from the partisans who'd planned to hang him from a lamppost. Then she'd hidden him on her farm, nursing him back to health.

A hand caressed his bearded cheek and a sleepy voice said, "Don't worry so much. We've made it until now, so we'll somehow survive this awful war."

"I wish you were right, my darling."

They didn't talk much, gathered their things, tied them into the shawl and took off toward Breslau again. He still doubted the wisdom of going there, but what else could they do?

For a moment he considered turning himself in to the Russian authorities, then Katrina might not be bothered. But as it did every German soldier, the *Russenschreck*, the Russian terror, scared him too much to actually pursue that idea.

Around noon, trudging along the only road leading west, they saw pillars of smoke billowing in the sky. Distant artillery fire vibrated through the air. A short time later they came upon a column of dirty, dejected and depleted German soldiers, looking like lambs being led to the slaughter.

Instinctively, he moved away from the road, his gaze glued to the earth in front of his shoes. Katrina took his hand in hers as if she sensed his fright. Any moment now, the Russian captors could demand his papers, and God only knew whether they'd believe he was an innocent Pole.

Thankfully, the Russian soldiers were too busy herding the captured men forward to pay attention to a couple dressed in rags. Since fleeing Mrs. Jaworski's ruined farm, they hadn't been able to pick up any information about the current state of war. He itched to know what news the captured men had, but didn't dare ask.

Katrina, though, wasn't as scrupulous as he was and when one of the soldiers fell, she approached the column, helping him up. Moments later one of the guards appeared by her side, cursing her in Russian and telling her to back off.

When the column of prisoners was out of sight, Richard said, "You shouldn't endanger yourself like that."

"I had to. The German soldier told me they've been fighting a few miles away from Breslau. The entire region is in Russian hands, save for the city itself. Fortress Breslau, as he called it, has been under siege by the Red Army for weeks. Hitler has given the order to defend it at all cost."

"Hitler is fond of these suicide missions defending whatever point he deems strategic, sacrificing thousands of men in the process," Richard said with a bitter tone. He'd been on the receiving side of those ludicrous orders many a time.

She sighed. "We may not be able to get to my relatives."

"I thought they lived in a village nearby, not in the city itself?"

"They do. Or at least they did last time I heard from them, but the only road to go there is through Breslau, which we can't do at the moment." They continued to walk in silence for quite a while before Katrina raised her voice again. "What do we do now?"

"We need to eat."

"I know."

About an hour later they came upon an isolated farm

that seemed unaffected by the fighting and he said, "We could ask to work in exchange for food. This farm looks like they might need helping hands."

"We can try, but you let me do the talking," she said as they approached the farmhouse.

Richard knocked at the door and when an ancient man came outside, Katrina said, "Mister, we're seeking to reunite with family in Breslau—"

"It's under siege. No way to get in or out," the old man answered.

"We heard, so now we don't know where to go and were wondering if you'd allow us to work in exchange for food and shelter for the night? We both know about farm work and aren't lazy."

The old man cast a suspicious glance at her and Richard before he nodded. "In fact, I have a lot more work than these old hands can do. See that pile of wood over there? Chop and stack it and my wife will bring you dinner at night. You can sleep over there in the shed."

"*Dziękuję!*" Richard thanked him with a hoarse voice to hide his accent, before he turned on his heels and started chopping the wood, while Katrina stacked it neatly.

Hours later, his stomach growling louder than an approaching tank, he said, "Let's hope dinner is worth it."

When they finished just after darkness settled over the land, the farmer's wife arrived with a steaming pot and two wooden spoons. "We don't have much, but that should fill your stomachs."

"Thank you," Katrina said, before they hurriedly spooned the hot stew into their mouths. It was mostly hot water, but contained pieces of potato and carrot and some meager chicken bones. After finishing their meal they returned the dishes to the farmhouse and the lady gave them two thick blankets to make a bed in the shed. After wrapping themselves in the blankets, it was surprisingly warm inside the shed, even though fierce winds howled outside.

"We could stay here for a while," Richard suggested, reaching for Katrina. "At least until we can find a way to get to your relatives."

Katrina leaned against him. The warmth of her soft body chased away his exhaustion and he proceeded to undress her and make sweet love to her.

CHAPTER 3

Waking up without her bones chilled to ice was a welcome change, and Katrina decided to proceed with Richard's suggestion and ask the farmer for more work. Since they couldn't reach her mother's cousin, they might as well stay here until the damned war was finally over.

Indeed, there was more than enough to do, and the farmer seemed pleased with yesterday's work and offered to extend the deal. Now, in mid-April, when the snow had melted from the fields, it was time to prepare for the planting season.

"You can start ploughing the fields," the old man said, pointing at the plow under a roof behind the shed.

"What about the tractor?" Richard eyed the rusty vehicle in a corner of the yard.

"No fuel. And no animals. You have to do it yourselves."

Katrina saw the resignation in Richard's eyes. Plowing

was backbreaking work with an ox to pull the heavy plough, and next to impossible with human power alone.

"We'll do it," she said.

Hours later, the sweat running down her back in rivulets, she pressed her hands on her hips and stretched out. Despite the feeble April sun and the low temperature she was burning up from the strenuous work.

"We haven't done much," Richard said, stepping beside her and looking down the field.

"No. That damn plough is too heavy and the earth is still hard from the frost."

"That's why mankind invented machinery to do it for them. But we have no choice. Let's continue."

Thus, they spent day after day consumed with grueling work and fell into an exhausted sleep the moment they'd eaten their evening meal. Sometimes they would see bedraggled refugees traveling west and columns of captured Wehrmacht soldiers marching east.

Richard stopped pulling the plough and looked at the lines of soldiers. "Do you think I'm a coward?"

"You? Why?" Katrina looked at him, tied together in that darned harness that should have been worn by two oxen or horses.

"Because I'm hiding out here. I should be with them." He nodded over to the captured Wehrmacht soldiers.

"You're not a coward. Remember that you asked to be transferred to the front line again, because you refused to commit the atrocious crimes against the civilians that were expected of you in Lodz?"

"Hmm." He fell in step again and whether she wanted to

or not, she had to follow his lead. "That still doesn't make it right. Fact is, I deserted. Any deserter is a coward."

This time, Katrina stopped and the jerk of the harness caused *him* to lose his step. "That's not true. You did a very heroic thing when you rescued my nephew and Agnieska."

"But why should I have it better than they do?" His voice sounded torn with self-doubt.

"Better? Look at us? We're replacing two oxen in this harness. Does that look like a life of luxury to you?" She wanted to joke, but looking at him, smeared with dirt and sweat from head to toe, the laughter caught in her throat.

"Hmm." He sighed and pulled at the harness again.

"Look, Richard, the war's not over yet and if either side found out you're a Wehrmacht soldier hiding in civilian clothes, you'd be shot on sight."

"I knew it!" An irate voice shouted at them, making Katrina's skin crawl. She slowly turned her head and looked into the furious face of the farmer's wife bringing them their lunch. "German bastards! You'd better leave my farm, before my husband kills you. Filthy rats!"

"Please, it's not what you think. I'm really a Pole, and he—"

"I've heard enough, you Nazi whore! Get off my land."

Accompanied by shouted profanities Richard and Katrina left the plough stuck in the hard dirt and hurried back to the shed to gather their meager belongings. The farmer, alerted by his wife, entered the shed with a pitch-fork. They split up, weaving around him on opposite sides, leaving him unsure of a strategy. That one moment allowed them enough time to slip out of the door and run for their lives until they reached the edge of the forest.

With a pounding heart, Katrina dropped on her knees, before she slumped to the ground, heaving gigantic mouthfuls of air.

"That was close," Richard murmured after a while. When she turned her head to look at him, she saw the worry in his face. "I was so scared he'd hurt you."

"Me? I was afraid he'd spear you with that pitchfork," she answered, still breathless.

Richard rolled over and took her into his arms. "You're still shaking," he said, rubbing a hand up and down her back.

"Now what?" she said with a feeble voice.

"We need to get away from this place."

"But where to?"

"I don't know." Richard squeezed her shoulders and then helped her up. They started walking without giving thought to the direction, just away from the hostile farmers.

"Stop!" Katrina said after about an hour of senseless walking. "We can't keep walking without sense and direction. We need a plan."

A half-smile appeared on Richard's lips and once again love flooded her heart. With him by her side, she could overcome anything.

"It's not safe for you here," she said.

"We'll walk further away…"

"No, I don't mean just in this place. We can't stay here in Poland. It's not safe for you. You've seen the hordes of German refugees fleeing the country." As the Russians gained ground, the Poles celebrated the liberation from the hated German oppressor and systematically freed each town of German influence. And it wasn't only the new German settlers that they chased away, but also the ones who'd been living in Poland for generations.

"I don't know what I would do if something happened to you," she said, holding back tears as raw emotion clogged her throat.

"Nothing is going to happen to me." Richard hugged her close, but she could still see the look of shame and guilt etched on his face. "I have forged Polish papers, so I will just have to be more careful. I'll keep away from groups of people and keep my head down. I promise to not to speak German anymore. From now on I'll be one hundred percent Polish. Just like you."

He pressed a kiss on her lips and Katrina couldn't help but soften against him. His kiss clouded her clear thinking; it had almost convinced her, when a nagging voice in her head forced her to push away from him.

"It's not just the language; it's also your accent. It's not Polish. It's not even close," Katrina said, hoping he'd see the danger of their present situation.

"So, what do you recommend?"

"Let me do the talking from now on," Katrina suggested.

"Won't that be suspicious? I'm the man so I am supposed to do the talking."

"We could tell them your voice is damaged. If you can't help talking, do it coughing and with a raspy voice. That should help conceal your accent."

He grinned. "I always knew you wanted to have a say, and this is just a ruse."

"Richard! I'm dead serious," she protested.

"I know, darling. And if it puts your mind at ease, you can do all the talking for both of us. You'll see, we'll be just fine."

"That still leaves us with the question of where to go."

"We could return to your farm in Lodz." Richard's suggestion almost broke her heart. She yearned to return to her home, but that wouldn't be feasible for as long as the Nazis lingered.

"It's too dangerous. We have to wait out the war first."

"Well, despite everyone knowing it'll end soon, it could still take months. So what do we do in the meanwhile?" Richard said, running a hand through his short blond hair.

"We could try to find a way around Breslau and get to my relatives..."

"Or we wait. The siege cannot go on forever. You could ask around in some of the villages. Maybe someone knows about your family."

"So Breslau it is." Katrina looked at the position of the sun in the sky and checked the time on her wristwatch. Then she pointed behind them. "That's west. We need to get out of the forest and find a road that leads west."

Once they reached the main road, they joined the never-ending trek of German refugees traveling west. Despite the temptation to stay with a bigger group, they kept their distance, making sure they walked out of earshot of other people.

"Look, Richard, how beautiful," she said with a smile, pointing at white and blue wildflowers that had miraculously survived the trampling hordes of soldiers and fugitives crossing the war-torn country.

"Flowers," he said with an indulgent smile.

"Beautiful remnants of better times." She bent down to appreciate the simple yet miraculous life. A bright spot of color in an otherwise gray and dreary world. She reached out her hand to pick the delicate blue and fragile flowers, but then hesitated, her hand hovering inches above the blossoms. While she wanted to keep their beauty with her for just a little while longer, she hated to condemn them to a quick death by her hand. So she glanced at the flowers twinkling in the sunlight and then stood up again, empty-handed.

"Katrina?" Richard's insistent voice brought her back to the present.

She sighed. "When is this going to end?"

He reached for her hand. "Soon. Keep your spirits up. I know it seems like this war has been going on forever, but the end is near. I can smell defeat in the air."

"Defeat?" she giggled. "What you're smelling is artillery smoke."

"That... and defeat. I was in the Wehrmacht long enough to know how soldiers look when they know it's over. I saw it in the eyes of the Russians for two years, and now I'm seeing it in the eyes of the captured Germans."

"Of course the prisoners look defeated. For them it's over and they're marching into an uncertain future."

"It's not just that. I can't explain it, but their expressions make it clear it's not simply a lost battle, the entire war is lost."

"Let's hope you're right. I sure would love to live in peace again and return to our farm." Katrina was setting one foot in front of the other, not really paying attention to the road, when they rounded a curve and suddenly saw the stronghold of Breslau looming in the distance.

"Oh my God!" She stopped in her tracks, a queasiness taking hold of her stomach.

CHAPTER 4

"There's no way we can go there," Richard said, taking a deep breath. Even from this far away the image of destruction cloaked him in a wave of depression. And the putrid stink of rotting corpses, burning ashes and acrid gunpowder made him gag.

Nothing had prepared them for the sight before their eyes. He could sense how Katrina recoiled from the impact. The road ahead was filled with equally disturbed people, who now turned around to find a way to bypass the city on their westward trek.

"Let's find out what's going on," Katrina suggested.

"And how?"

Displaced persons like them milled about the roadway, along with Russian soldiers going back and forth between their camp and the besiegement girdle with the heavy weaponry.

"Let's ask one of the soldiers," Katrina suggested.

"That's too dangerous. We'd better return to the last

village we passed through; maybe someone knows more."

Katrina nodded, and they backtracked about an hour until they came upon a small village.

"You stay back, I'll go and ask," she said.

Richard wanted to protest, but he understood that danger lurked and didn't press the issue. Alone, she could talk with the locals without raising suspicions. Still, he sat there, on tenterhooks until she finally returned an hour later.

"It's bad. Real bad. Nobody can get in or out. The radio says the Germans are building a runway for aircraft to relieve them. But it's only a matter of time until they have to give up. For weeks now, no food has gotten inside." She swallowed. "A farmer said there's no road to get to the village of my relatives, except through Breslau."

"We could walk through the forest…"

"No, it's on the other side of the Oder, and there's only one bridge left. He said many refugees have tried rowing boats or even swimming, but due to the snowmelt and heavy rains it's not possible."

He put a hand on her arm, not sure what to say.

"One man in the village offered us shelter in his barn. It's far enough away so you won't have to talk to anyone."

"You want to wait here until the siege is over?"

"What else can we do?" she said, suddenly sounding tired.

"Not much. Although the chances of finding your family are slim, and we might be better off moving on." His heart broke at the devastated expression on her face when she took in the import of his words.

"But where would we go?"

It plagued him that he didn't have a ready answer for even that simple question. In fact, there was no place they could go. As long as the war raged on, he was a wanted person. His forged papers might be good enough for some disinterested patrol in the countryside, but not for the SS border patrol. He'd be shot or hanged the instant he set foot into the Reich.

On the other hand, he couldn't stay in Poland either. People were already being scrutinized more carefully than before and as Katrina had pointed out, his accent belied his fake identity with every word he uttered. Hiding out in a barn seemed to be the best of possibilities.

"We'll wait," Richard said after another glance at Katrina's dirty and tired face.

"We'll wait," she whispered and picked up the handmade backpack to hand it to him before she led the way to the barn the man had offered them. "I'm so tired and worried that I just want to lie down and forget."

Richard hugged her close. "I know. That seems to be the only thing we can count on each day. Being tired and worried." He almost added hungry to the list, but he and Katrina had an unspoken pact not to mention that topic as it only made their burning stomachs harder to endure.

As April drew to an end and May arrived with warming sunshine, more and more displaced persons on their way to Breslau arrived and then turned away in defeat, not able to get inside the besieged city or through it. The caravan of bedraggled people changed direction, looking for a way around the besieged city, their ultimate destination relative safety within the new, narrower borders of Germany.

Nobody knew what would happen, but everyone knew

they couldn't stay in the places they'd called home for generations.

Richard and Katrina, though, settled into a daily life of scavenging for food in the fields and the woods. Many fields had lost their owners to the war and the two of them weren't the only ones to dig with their bare hands in the hard earth for forgotten potatoes from last year. Katrina sometimes talked to the locals, but Richard always kept to himself, aware that his disguise wouldn't hold up under closer inspection.

As he stood to stretch, his gaze fell on the columns of smoke hovering over the city like demons ready to sweep down. He bit down a sarcastic remark. The sorrow-stricken inhabitants probably had greater problems than a random demon.

"There are more fires and more smoke every day," he said.

Katrina nodded. "The villagers say the Germans are bombing their own strongholds and are blowing up the buildings that have survived the Russian attacks. They lined that damn runway with the lives of hundreds of the children they forced to build it, while the Russian strafers hunted them like rabbits."

He saw her fighting against her tears and put an arm around her shoulders. Only rare news came from the besieged city, and it was never good.

Most of the intelligence came from Red Army aircraft strafing the city beneath. Richard was well aware that the information Katrina received over the neighborly gossip network was highly controlled and filtered. The Soviets would only divulge what benefited them. They controlled not only the air space, but also the perimeter around the city, shooting anyone attempting to flee and stopping those wanting to go inside.

"Apparently, Nazi Gauleiter Hanke publicly hanged the mayor of Breslau, because he opposed the demolition of irreplaceable cultural heritages like libraries, churches and mansions to create open fighting areas," Katrina continued.

"Hanke is one of the worst," Richard said. "They call him The Hangman of Breslau, because he ordered the execution of more than one thousand people as soon as he arrived in the city. When I was still in the Wehrmacht, even the most hardened soldiers would shudder at his merciless cruelty." A shiver racked Katrina's body and he pressed her tighter against himself. "It'll all be over soon."

"We've been hoping for this for such a long time. Sometimes I think it will never end, and every day I'm afraid we'll die before it does." She leaned into him, her dirty face pressed into his chest.

"You cannot lose hope. I promise, we will survive this war."

"How can you promise such a thing?" she asked, looking up at him with defeat in her eyes. He simply had to sweep away the sadness and make her laugh, and he already knew how.

"You can hold me personally responsible for lying if we both die," he said with a smug grin.

His words had the intended effect and she showed him her white teeth as she broke out in laughter. "You know that you're hilarious, right?"

"I'd do anything to make you smile," he said, wondering whether he should kiss her or let her continue laughing. He opted for the latter. Seeing a laugh on her beautiful face had become such a rare occasion since they'd had to flee Mrs. Jaworski's farm that he wanted to savor it. Treasure it like one of the exquisite blue blossoms she hadn't had the heart to pick.

"How do you do it?" she asked.

"Do what?"

"Make it seem that life is easy."

Richard paused for a moment. "I guess... since I cannot change my surroundings, I can at least change my way of looking at them. And there's always something beautiful in every situation."

"Thank you," she whispered, pressing a kiss on his lips, until a particularly ferocious blast in the distance shook the earth and parted them. Looking up into the reddish sky over Breslau where smoke billowed, Richard noticed an aircraft taking off in their direction, before it curved and flew southward.

"It's a Fieseler Storch," Richard said, wondering what that might mean. Had the Germans found a way to evacuate the city? Would the Russians allow this to happen? They had total air superiority and it seemed peculiar that they allowed an aircraft to take off, despite its being only a small liaison plane that was usually unarmed and primarily used to transport commanding officers or urgent messages. Capitulation negotiators maybe?

"What does this mean?" Katrina asked as she shadowed her eyes and watched the aircraft flying into the sun before it curved yet again and headed westward.

"I don't know, but I guess we'll soon find out."

Only minutes later, a boy of about six years came

running from the village shouting at the top of his lungs. "The Nazis surrendered! Breslau is free!"

Richard couldn't believe his ears. But the boy held a small battery-run radio in his hands and one by one the people digging in the fields approached him to hear the announcement in Polish and Russian.

Over the next days more and more information reached them. Apparently, a delegation of both the Catholic and Protestant churches had urged the commanding general Niehoff to negotiate the capitulation. SS-Obergruppen-führer Hanke, though, the cruel leader of the NSDAP in Breslau, had insisted on sacrificing every last human being under his care on the altar of cultish obedience to a lunatic Führer and his ideas of racial superiority.

But when the Red Army marched into the defeated city, Hanke was nowhere to be found. It soon became obvious that in the last moments of the fight when he'd demanded the human sacrifice of thousands, he'd finally shown his true colors and fled the place in the Fieseler Storch aircraft Richard had seen take off.

"We need to go and find my relatives," Katrina said on the second day.

"That's crazy. You've heard what's happening in there."

"We'll rapidly walk through the city, nobody will bother us," she answered, pushing out her lower lip in that stubborn way of hers. He sighed, knowing she wasn't willing to discuss this topic any further.

"Let's at least wait until the morning."

She cast him a dark stare. "You won't change my mind. I'll go in the morning, whether you come with me or not."

"I'll come with you alright."

CHAPTER 5

Early the next morning Katrina packed their things, unswayed by Richard's dour face and his incessant attempts to persuade her to change her mind.

"Richard, I have to go. What if they need help?"

"What kind of help can we offer? We have nothing…" He bit on his lip, his jaw tense, and she had to suppress a smile at the amount of self-restraint he exercised not to blow up at her. She could understand him, partly.

It was an outright dangerous, even insane, undertaking to cross the freshly liberated stronghold to find her relatives. But in this ugly war where so many had died, she would feel like a fraud if she didn't go above and beyond to help a friend who might be in need. For all she knew, their village could have been bombed to the ground during the siege.

"Look. What would you do if it was your family?"

"That's different…" He didn't finish his sentence, probably aware that it wasn't different at all. She might not be close to her mother's cousin, she might not have seen them in years, but they were still family.

Katrina laid a hand upon his arm. "Please come with me."

He nodded and minutes later they left the barn, looking back one last time at their temporary home. The road was filled with streams of fugitives leaving the city and others wanting to get inside. She couldn't wrap her head around the fact that half of the people were fleeing the place while the other half flocked to it. Were they all searching for relatives like she was? Or what did they hope to find in a city that had been besieged and brutally bombed for the past months?

Instinctively she put her hand into Richard's. She hadn't wanted to admit it, but fear tugged at every cell in her body. And she wasn't sure she could have mustered the courage to venture into the den of the lion without him by her side.

As they approached the city walls, the putrid stench in the air made her gag and she almost regretted her decision. Soviet soldiers manned the now open city gates, but the guard on duty gave their papers only a cursory glance.

The information they had gathered over the radio didn't reflect reality. Things were much worse than Katrina had dared to imagine.

The people milling about appeared to be the living dead: hollow-cheeked, dust-covered automatons. She searched their eyes for a trace of humanity, but only found wild madness or silent resignation.

Her heart pumping against the oppressive atmosphere, she murmured, "How can anyone still live here?"

"The human mind and body can endure much more

than we believe," Richard said. After one glance at the pained expression on his face she knew what he was thinking about. He'd never shared details of his experiences at the Eastern front with her, but she'd held him in her arms through countless nights filled with nightmares.

Putting one foot in front of the other, she frantically racked her brain, trying to remember how to get to her relatives' village that lay adjacent to the formerly beautiful city. Breslau had been nicknamed "Jewel at the Oder River" for its cultural heritage and splendor, but that was before the insidious war turned it into acres of scorched earth.

What used to be broad streets lined by pompous mansions were now empty fields of rubble, lined by rotting corpses and the ever-present rats and crows feasting on them.

Katrina brought a hand over her mouth, and Richard handed her a kerchief. "Here, breathe through this. It helps."

Unable to form a coherent thought, she obeyed and pressed the kerchief in front of mouth and nose. Katrina kept her eyes away from the ground, frantically looking for the bridge she knew they had to cross.

Her foot caught in something soft and she tripped, falling forward. Stiff as a poker, a bloodied corpse loomed at her and she opened her mouth for a silent cry. Just before the impact, two strong hands grabbed her shoulders and pulled her up again.

Heaving like a locomotive, her brain filled with torment, she leaned against Richard's hard chest.

"Let's get out of here," he said in a low voice, as if he were afraid to disturb the dead people lying about.

Katrina yearned to close her eyes to the awful scenes but

looking away had already made her stumble. If Richard hadn't saved her, she'd now be lying atop a half-rotten corpse. She cursed her stupid idea of crossing the city. But even in her worst nightmares she'd never have imagined the horrific destruction enveloping the city.

Finally she found the street leading to the Oder. Through the brownish, muddy river water, rubble crested the waves like little boats. On another day, the sight might have coaxed a smile or laugh, but today, she could only gape open-mouthed at the destroyed bridge that had been scantily repaired with wooden planks that looked like doors.

"I'm not going over that," she said as they reached the river.

"It's the bridge or return. We can't stay in the city."

She took a deep breath and willed away the images of herself falling into the cold water, being dragged away by the treacherous current and joining the piles of corpses. Then she looked at Richard, already heaving himself up onto the rickety bridge and extending his hand to help her up.

Dear goodness, what did I sign up for with my stubbornness? She grabbed his hand and followed him up on the bridge. The first steps were wobbly, but not too scary with the comforting bank beneath. But at the point where the bridge extended across the swooshing and hissing water, an icy fear trickled down her body, making her knees tremble and her balance shaky. She stuck to the thicker beams and tried to convince herself the dangerous journey involved nothing more than walking on a curbstone, but a slurping sound made her look down at the water. Moments later she saw something bump hard against a pillar nearest to her. A startled shout escaped her throat and she had to pinwheel her arms to regain her balance.

"Come on, it gets better over here," Richard yelled at her.

She narrowed her eyes at his obvious lie. When she reached him, he stood on the other side of a big, gaping hole in the structure.

"You have to jump."

"I'm not gonna jump."

"Come on. You can do this. It's not that far and I'll catch you."

"Yes, and then we'll both fall into the Oder."

"At least we'll sink together. Remember, if we both die, you can blame me." He grinned at her with that boyish charm she so loved. *What does he think? That this is a child's game? Jumping from rock to rock, and whoever doesn't lose their footing wins?*

"I don't plan on dying in the icy waters."

"Neither do I, and now jump!"

She took one last breath, defied the gurgling water beneath her and… jumped. High in the air, she saw the planks on the other side of the hole coming closer and closer. With exasperation she shoved her arms and legs forward they way she'd seen broad jumpers do it and finally felt Richard's hands grab her wrists, a split second before her feet hit the wooden planks.

She fell into his arms, cold with fright, but also proud at the accomplished task.

"See, I told you, you could do it." He grinned at her in such a smug way she forgot all about her fears and cast him a relieved smile. For now, she'd ignore his impertinence, but only because he'd saved her from falling into the cold water.

Conquering the rest of the bridge was a breeze. The scenery on the other side of the Oder wasn't any different, and she took a few minutes to regain her breath as soon as she stepped on solid ground. Due to her sketchy memory, nothing in the defeated city looked like it had many years ago, but she finally recognized a tall – yet half destroyed – tower that must be the western city gate. Just beyond that gate, a fifteen-minute walk led to her relatives' village.

If it still existed.

If *they* still existed.

"Over there." She pointed at the tower and wound her way through streets filled with rubble and human remains.

With a deep sigh she left the destroyed city behind and walked to the adjacent village. The situation wasn't much better there, either. Soviet troops had trampled back and forth across the land in their quest to conquer the besieged stronghold.

As they arrived at the village, they found the houses still intact, but requisitioned first by the Germans and now by the Red Army. She asked around for her relatives. Richard always kept behind, loitering as if he didn't belong.

After several vain attempts a kind old woman finally recognized the names of Katrina's relatives and led them to a disused sewer outlet, where several Polish families had dug out a meager existence.

Katrina swallowed hard at the hostile surroundings, thinking it impossible that such a place could be used as housing. She ventured inside the network of tunnels that lay dry since the sewage system had been destroyed.

An old man stepped up to her, asking with an unfriendly face, "What do you want here?"

"I'm looking for my mother's cousin, Barbara Adamski. Does she live here?"

The man gave her a suspicious look and said, "Maybe. What do you want?"

"I'm looking for survivors. She's family," Katrina insisted.

"He your husband?" the man asked, nodding at Richard, who lingered about fifty feet back.

"No. He's a cousin from up North."

"Come. Both of you," he said and turned, leading them deeper into the labyrinth of tunnels.

Despite the unsavory prior use, the concrete structures were dry and offered shelter from the elements. The sunlight streaming in through the open manholes dimly lit the space and Katrina found it amazing how the families living here had converted the area into homes. Living quarters were separated by makeshift walls of cardboard, paper and wooden planks, equipped with mattresses, candles and even furniture.

"Barbara, there's someone to see you," the old man said, stopping at one of the makeshift apartments.

A frail woman in her late forties with her gray hair in a tight bun stood and approached them. "Oh, goodness! Katrina! Is that really you?" She wrapped Katrina into her arms before she glanced at Richard. "And this is?"

"A cousin from my father's side. His name is Ryszard Blach."

Barbara raised an eyebrow, seemingly aware of the slight tremble in Katrina's voice. Thankfully she didn't express her doubt, and acknowledged him, "Good day, cousin Ryszard."

Richard mumbled something that sounded like good day and shuffled to the wall.

"I'm sorry, he's not himself since his family was murdered. He rarely speaks."

Barbara gave a pensive nod before she smiled at Katrina, asking, "How's your mother?"

"Dead." Katrina's voice was laced thick with emotion. "Father, too. And Jarek. Stan's been taken prisoner of war and we still haven't had word about Piotr."

"Poor girl." Barbara didn't dwell on grief. Apparently, she'd had her share of deceased family members, too. "So what brings you into this little hell on earth?"

"Ryszard and I were living with a friend, but her farm became the main battleground and she got killed. We escaped, thinking we might..." Katrina looked around at the dreadful concrete tunnels. "...we might live with you. For a while. But I see how that's not possible."

"Of course, it's possible. Our home was requisitioned years ago and we moved into empty housing inside the city perimeter. Thankfully, my Edmund was wise enough to move us here before the Red Army closed the siege. It's not much, but you're welcome to stay with as for as long as you need. This war can't go on forever, now can it?"

"Thank you so much, Barbara. We appreciate your offer."

"You'll have to sleep on the ground, but it's dry in here and you're safe from marauding troops and vagrants."

Katrina looked to Richard, who pressed out a coarse "Thank you."

"We've been hiding in the forest for so long, this will feel like a castle." Katrina didn't mention the farmer who'd chased them away because Richard was German. Even though she trusted her relatives, she thought it prudent to keep up appearances and let them believe he was a Pole.

Much later, when everyone was asleep, Katrina and Richard huddled together on a blanket Barbara had given them and whispered into each other's ears.

"I don't like this man who brought us here, he smells of trouble," she said with a slight shiver.

"Your imagination is too vivid. He's just protective of the families living down here," Richard said, pressing his big hand on the skin of her back. She relished the feelings he evoked in her body, but with so many people sleeping – and snoring – all around them she couldn't relax into the feeling.

"Even Barbara is suspicious of you. She doesn't believe the cousin-from-up-North ruse."

"How do you know?" His hand insistently worked its way to the swell of her breasts while his lips nibbled on her earlobe.

"I just know. It was the glint in her eyes when I said cousin." Katrina could barely keep her thoughts together as his fingers drew circles on her naked skin. "Stop. Not here."

He gave a disappointed growl but obeyed and moved his hand once again to her backside. As if this would help to gather her wits.

"She's suspicious of your accent, too."

"I barely talked."

"Best to keep it that way. Pretend you're this strange maverick who lost his wits when his family perished."

Richard whispered into her ear, "I'll do anything to keep

us safe. But I don't like staying here. This place is a trap with no way out but the main entrance."

"We'll figure something out tomorrow." Katrina yawned and wrapped herself into Richard's arms. "Now let's get some sleep."

CHAPTER 6

Three days later, Germany capitulated and the war finally ended. Richard gave a huge sigh; maybe now everything would get better.

He and Katrina ventured out into the city of Breslau, looking for work, or food, or... anything. But they found... nothing.

The city lay moribund, the infrastructure in ruins and the inhabitants scurrying like rats to vacuum up morsels of food. The incessant bombing had left the dying city without hospitals, waterworks or even a sewer system.

Richard scrunched up his nose at the stink of a man relieving himself right there on the street for everyone to see and smell. The man seemed to suffer from diarrhea and when Richard noticed red dots on his half-exposed back, he took Katrina aside. "That looks an awful lot like typhus. We should get out of here."

"I wouldn't be surprised. With the unhygienic conditions in here and the lack of proper food and medication it was only a matter of time before the first disease broke out."

"Can't we return to your farm, now that the war is over?" He dreaded the hundred-mile walk back, but it was the safest place to be. *If* the farm still existed.

"It's something we can try." Katrina agreed with him, but he could see by the frown on her forehead that she didn't like the idea.

They walked to the next corner and saw a bunch of people tearing down street signs and shop signs, talking in rapid-fire Polish he didn't understand. They threw the signs onto a pile with books, gramophone records and German flags, gripped by an iconoclastic fury as the hatred against anything German burst free.

"What the hell are they doing?" Richard mumbled. He wanted to approach the group, but felt Katrina's hand on his arm.

"Don't."

"Why not? They're destroying what little is left of the city."

She gave a deep sigh and said, "They're taking down anything and everything that reminds them of the Germans. Doing drastic things like that is cathartic for them."

"But this city has been of German heritage for centuries." Richard felt a queasiness roil his stomach as he saw someone mount a sign that said *Wroclaw Registry. Poles only.* In their quest to rid the city they had stolen from Germany of every trace of the former population, the new administration had renamed the city from Breslau to Wroclaw, and continued to rename every street, place, shop, and church with Polish names.

Over the next days an influx of Poles being resettled from the eastern lands of Poland that now suddenly belonged to Russia were expected, and the autochthonous German population had to leave.

Moments later a young man bumped into him and Richard felt the cold blade of a knife pressed against his side.

"Give me your jacket," the thief demanded.

Richard gazed at the frightened face of the man dressed in rags. The youth looked about his age but was at least half a head shorter and incredibly skinny. Despite the pity he felt for the desperate boy, he wouldn't hand over the only jacket he owned.

"Alright, lad," he said and raised his hands. Katrina's eyes widened with horror as she grasped the situation and he mouthed a silent "run" in her direction. Then he turned in a swift move and grabbed the thief's hand with all his might.

The thief let out a cry and the knife fell to the ground. Richard kicked it away with his foot so Katrina could pick it up. Then he shoved the thief to the ground, took Katrina's hand and ran.

When they dared to stop, he looked at her, his decision made. He would not return to the city now named Wroclaw.

"Let's go to the tunnels," Katrina said. "We're not safe here."

In front of the entrance to the tunnels, they met Barbara waving at them with a proud expression. "We've found a new home to live!"

"Great. Where?"

"Pack your things and come with us. We're just moving everything over there," Barbara's husband Edmund said.

Richard merely nodded and followed Katrina inside to pack the few things they owned. Barbara and Edmund waited for them, giddy like two adolescents.

"This way," Edmund said and led the way across the village to a row of tidy houses adjacent to the city wall. Miraculously, they stood sturdily without the least bit of damage, even the window panes were still intact.

"We have to share this house with two other families, but we secured one room on the ground floor for us alone." Barbara beamed and entered the hallway. Stairs led up to the second floor, but she stayed on the ground level and showed them the small space, consisting of a tiny toilet near the entrance and a huge kitchen that was destined to be the communal gathering and cooking place.

Richard peered at the laid table, a queasy feeling taking a hold of his stomach. The entire kitchen looked as if someone had lived in here for ages. But how could that be, when Barbara and the other families had just moved in?

He touched the big pot on the range. It was still warm.

"Isn't it wonderful? And wait until you see our private room!" Edmund said and opened the door on the other side of the small hallway, stepping into a big, fully furnished living room. The old sofa, coffee table and armchairs reminded Richard of his grandmother's place.

"This will be our living and sleeping room. After living so long in those tunnels, this seems like paradise. We'll no longer have to put up with the snoring of old Karol." Barbara kept on praising the virtues of her new home, but

Richard stopped listening the moment he saw a picture of a five-person family on the mantel piece. He stepped nearer and lifted the framed photograph depicting a man and a woman with three small, blond children.

Something about the image triggered him and he took a closer look until he finally realized it. The father of the family wore a Wehrmacht uniform. Hot jolts of rage ran through his veins as he turned around and said in an accusing tone, "You kicked out the family who owns this house to move in yourselves?"

"They were German," Edmund said.

"And that gives you the right to—" Richard stopped mid-sentence, because Katrina gave him an angry glare and stepped in front of him, saying, "I'm sorry, Ryszard always gets upset when something reminds him of how his family was evicted from their house. He'll calm down."

"He'd better," Edmund murmured and turned away to move the sofa, so they would have space to put their mattresses. But Barbara's gaze lingered on Richard and he sensed her suspicion as she scrutinized him.

He feared he'd given himself away with his short burst of temper. No Pole would be angry at the eviction of a German family from their home. For the rest of the day he kept his mouth shut and helped Barbara and Edmund to make themselves at home in the stolen house. He wondered what had happened to the German family.

The father probably was a prisoner of war now – or dead. The mother with her three small children was out somewhere fighting for survival. He balled his hands into fists, ready to barge outside and look for them. But there was nothing he could do. His own survival hung by a thin thread.

The times he and Katrina ventured out into the city, he was struck by the violence gaining momentum. Armed gangs roamed the streets, looting everything they found. He witnessed the lynchings and public hangings in Wroclaw. And every day the persecution of the German citizens became more fervent and the punishments more extreme. He looked away when men were beaten to death and women and children were led away to the cellars.

A small part of his brain understood the hatred of the Poles and their need for revenge, but the bigger part sought a reconciliation. Now that peace officially prevailed again in Europe, shouldn't the people return to their lives instead of hunting down those who'd done them wrong?

Of course, the real perpetrators like Gauleiter Hanke shouldn't get away with impunity, but was it necessary to punish those who hadn't committed atrocious crimes just because of their nationality? Should the former lady of this house be punished for being a supporter of the regime? Where should that line be drawn?

His head ached as he sought to solve the conundrum.

"What's wrong?" Katrina asked him more than once, but he couldn't even meet her eyes. Did she, too, believe it was alright to throw a mother and her children out of their home?

After taking supper with the two families who lived upstairs, everyone retreated to their rooms to sleep. When the noises faded, and the twilight fell over the land, Barbara closed the door to their room and said, "Isn't it about time you told us the truth about yourself, Ryszard Blach?"

Droplets of ice froze him in place and he felt a shiver running down his spine. Quickly assessing the situation, he noticed no escape route. Edmund stood in front of the only window and Barbara blocked the door. Katrina walked up to him and put her hand around his waist.

"He's my boyfriend."

"I noticed as much, but that doesn't explain his love for the Germans." Barbara cast an accusatory glare at Katrina.

"And his very German accent," Edmund said.

Richard's heart pounded so loudly against his ribs, he barely heard their words. He held his tongue, struggling not to defend himself, knowing if he did it would only worsen the dangerous situation.

"He has Polish papers. I can show them to you," Katrina said in a desperate attempt to save his cover.

"Wouldn't be the first man with forged papers. A coward trying to evade war captivity?"

"I'm not a coward!" Richard stepped forward. "It is true; I'm German. I was in the Wehrmacht."

His confession brought expressions of shock and anger to the faces of Barbara and Edmund, but before they could utter a word, he said, "Please, let me explain. More than one year ago I deserted, because I didn't want to be part of the atrocities against civilians committed in Lodz."

"How convenient." Edmund spit on the floor. "It's still a cowardly thing to do."

"Richard is no coward – he rescued my nephew Janusz and my sister-in-law Agnieska from the Ghetto."

A glimmer of admiration appeared on Barbara's face as she said, "Piotr's son? With that Jewish girl? What was her name again?"

"Ludmila," Katrina answered.

"What happened to her?"

"She died early on of sickness in the Ghetto. Her sister Agnieska took care of Janusz. Richard got them out just before the Ghetto was closed and everyone transferred to Chelmno."

At the mention of Chelmno a visible shudder went through Barbara's body. She moved away from the door, taking a few tentative steps toward Richard. "Is this true?"

"Yes, it is. After that I couldn't return to the Wehrmacht. Katrina hid me on her farm."

"Please, Barbara, Edmund. I know this is a lot to ask, but will you keep Richard's identity a secret? You know what will happen to him if the mob discovers his true heritage."

"He'll be killed," Edmund stated plainly. "And God knows, he deserves it. Only a dead German is a good German."

Richard once again assessed the situation. The Adamskis had lost two sons to the war, a third one still missing. Edmund was eaten up by hate for the Germans. Now that Barbara wasn't blocking the door anymore he could run for it. But how far would he get? It would take Edmund less than ten seconds to rush outside and scream, *Stop him, he's a German.* No, flight wasn't the answer. He was completely and utterly at the mercy of the Adamskis.

"Please, Barbara. For the sake of family. For my mother," Katrina pleaded with them. Richard saw how the stern expression on Barbara's face softened and she finally said, "Alright. But we'll deny any knowledge should he be found out."

"Thank you." Katrina wrapped her arms around her mother's cousin. "We'll be careful, I promise."

"Thank you," Richard said.

A wave of relief flowed over him as the immediate danger abated, but a sense of foreboding nagged at him. Deep in his heart, he knew it.

Trouble was coming.

CHAPTER 7

K atrina lay on the sofa, Richard on the floor at her side, and she sensed the tension and worry that consumed him, even as he seemed to sleep. From the other side of the room came the steady breathing of the others. But they weren't filled with anguish and fear.

After the mob hunts and lynchings she'd been witnessing, Katrina already knew that remaining in Wroclaw wasn't safe for Richard. Today's events had only been the last straw, further fortifying her decision that they needed to leave as soon as possible. Not only for his sake, but also for her own and the safety of the Adamskis. Anyone suspected of collaborating with the Germans awaited the same fate as the hated enemy.

In the wee hours of the night, Richard stirred and rolled to face her. "You haven't slept all night, have you?"

"No. I'm worried," she whispered.

"I know. We need to leave this place. I don't want to put Barbara and Edmund in danger."

"And go where?"

"Someplace where the two of us can live together in peace."

Katrina suppressed a sharp laugh. "And just where would that be? Also, how do you suppose we get there?"

"What if we return to your farm? We lived there unbothered for a year." Richard took her hand in his.

"No. It's too dangerous. People in Lodz will hate the Germans the same way they do here. We'll live in the same fear that someone will find out your papers are forged."

"Then what should we do? Where can we go?" His whisper took on a desperate tone.

"We need to leave Poland." The moment she said it, nostalgia burdened her heart. Could she really leave her home, her fatherland, her culture – possibly forever?

Richard squeezed her hand for several long moments. Both lost in their thoughts, they tried desperately to come up with a solution. Then he said, "I'm afraid you're right. The only safe place for me is Germany."

"You want to go to Germany?" Katrina asked.

"It doesn't matter if I want to or not. I'm afraid it's the only choice I have. If I stay here, it's only a matter of time before someone finds out just like your relatives already did."

Katrina swallowed hard. She had seen firsthand what happened to the Germans who couldn't flee fast enough. Those hanged on lampposts were the lucky ones. The ones taken to camps were given bitter mouthfuls from their own cookbook of violence and torture. She shivered at the mental images of what she knew and what was rumored.

"I don't want you to die," Katrina whispered.

"Me, either." He managed to give her a grin. "The faster we leave the better. Your relatives are in danger as long as we stay here." He tugged hard at her hand and, unprepared for the impact, she rolled off the sofa and onto him. His grin broadened into a cheeky smile as he wrapped his arms around her and kissed her lips. "I love you, my sweet woman."

"I love you, too." She pulled down the blanket from the sofa and draped it over both of them as she snuggled against Richard's warm body and soon fell into an exhausted sleep. Once they had left Poland behind, Richard would be safe again.

~

In the morning, they told Barbara and Edmund.

"We have come to the conclusion that it's best for me to leave," Richard said, sitting at the coffee table with a mug of hot, slightly flavored water that Barbara had called *tea*.

"That's a good idea," Edmund said, the relief clearly showing on his expression.

"When are you leaving?" Barbara settled on the sofa beside her husband.

"We will leave as soon as possible, probably tomorrow," Katrina said.

Barbara's head jerked around, the shock written all over her face. "We? You plan to go with him?"

"Of course. He's the man I love."

"Think about it. You're not safe with him," Barbara implored, putting a hand on Katrina's arm. "What would your mother say, if she knew you're risking your life for this man?"

"She'd probably congratulate me on loving such a wonderful man. He'll protect me and I'll protect him."

Katrina stubbornly put out her lower lip. Her relatives might think otherwise, but she intended to stick with Richard through thick and thin.

"His very existence is a threat to you. If he's captured, you'll go down with him. If not for being a German, then for being a collaborator."

"I don't care. I'm going with him," Katrina declared. "We're together. Certainly you can understand that."

Barbara cursed beneath her breath and then directed her attention to Richard. "Ryszard, you can't allow this. Talk some sense into her."

"I agree that she's safer with you, but it's her choice, not mine."

"You can't be serious! If you care for her at all, convince her to stay here with us," Barbara insisted.

Her husband quickly added, "Order her to stay."

Katrina's brow furrowed. Edmund was a good man, but he had very traditional values. In his opinion a wife had to obey her husband, a daughter her father or brother. And a single woman like her the man who was assigned to take care of her, which right now seemed to be Richard.

"I'm going. And that's my last word," Katrina said, a trace too loud.

"Where are you headed?" Barbara asked on a sigh.

"Berlin," Richard said.

Silence ensued while the shock waves travelled across

the room, until Barbara found her voice again. "That's in Germany. You can't be serious!"

"I am serious. My family lives in Berlin and despite everything, we'll be safe once we reach Germany."

"No way. I'm not allowing you to take Katrina with you into enemy country. We haven't fought this bloody war against the Nazi swine just so you can come here and take our girls away with you. She's a Pole! She stays here!" Edmund all but shouted.

Katrina turned her head toward the footfalls in the hallway outside their room and said, "No need to shout; you'll wake up the neighbors."

Edmund glared daggers at her, but kept his mouth shut. He was as afraid as Katrina to be ratted out for hiding a German.

"Look, Edmund, I understand your concern, but you know how stubborn Katrina can be. If she wants to come with me, there's nothing I can do or say to change her mind. But I will do everything in my power to protect her. We'll both be safe once we reach Berlin."

"You'll have your hands full protecting yourself," Edmund said in a low growling voice. "She stays here."

"I'm standing right here and I can make my own decisions." Katrina took a step forward and put her hands on her hips.

"Katrina, please be reasonable. Stay here. With us. In a few months, after things settle down, he can tell you where he ended up and you two can see one another again," Barbara pleaded with her.

Katrina shook her head in disbelief. "Would you leave

Edmund if the situations were reversed? Would you take the risk that you might never see each other again?"

Barbara didn't answer and Katrina took her own cues. She would stay by Richard's side, come hell or high water.

"Silly girl. Your parents would be turning in their graves if they knew what you were doing," Barbara said as she gathered the dishes from the coffee table. "I have to go to the market and will be gone most of the day."

"I'm going to work," Edmund growled. "The two of you better have a plan ready by tonight."

Katrina sagged with relief when the two left the room and she walked over to Richard and wrapped her arms around him. "Now what?"

CHAPTER 8

"Now we plan our escape," Richard said, pressing Katrina's tiny body against his. It was the first time in weeks that the two of them were alone. "But first I need to make love to you."

"What, now? It's broad daylight and we should go out and prepare for our journey," she protested.

He didn't care. He'd suppressed his desire for weeks, and who knew when they'd be alone again, within the reach of a soft mattress in a dry place. He walked over to the door and locked it, before he returned to his woman, who'd given up protesting, because she'd missed making love as much as he had.

He slowly undressed her, more in love with her than ever before. "You don't have to flee with me, you know that?" he murmured, caressing her soft skin. "This journey will be dangerous and we don't know what we'll find once we get to Berlin."

"I'd rather die by your side than live without you." Her answer warmed his heart, and he looked down into her eyes, kissing her tenderly. His second kiss was filled with more passion, and his third had both of them gasping quietly for breath and trying to calm their racing hearts.

Within seconds he forgot about threats and dangers and concentrated solely on her body and the pleasure both of them experienced in each other's arms. He held her gaze as he slowly made love to her, searing this moment forever into his brain, soul and heart.

Later, Richard held her against his chest and said, "Maybe your friends are right and you should stay with them."

"No. They are not. We are better off together. Besides, if we separate now, we might never find each other again."

He knew he should insist, implore, and beg for her to stay here. But the truth was, he didn't want to be without her, either.

"Are you sure this is what you want?" Richard asked, pulling her closer.

"I'm sure. My home is wherever you are."

"I will always love you." He kissed her hands, before he continued, "Görlitz is the new border town between Poland and Germany." Richard's blood still boiled at the accomplished facts Stalin had created, taking a big chunk of German territories and giving it to Poland, while at the same time declaring huge areas in Poland's East as Russian.

"We need to find out how to get there," Katrina said and slipped from his embrace. They both stood and dressed, before she searched the bookshelf in the room and then approached him with a huge smile. "Look what I found!"

"An atlas. In German."

They found Görlitz on the map and calculated it was about one hundred miles west of Wroclaw.

"We can walk this in a week," Richard said, excitement taking hold of him. After years away he'd finally return to Germany. And, what was even more important, within a week's time he wouldn't have to hide behind forged papers anymore and he'd be safe.

"Let's stock up on food to take."

"And pay for it how?"

"With this." Katrina took the framed picture of the former owners from the mantelpiece. "That's silver and will bring a good price on the black market."

Richard wanted to knock the object out of her hand, but much to his dismay he knew she was right. The owners were gone, possibly dead, never to come back to claim what was theirs. The silver frame would ensure he and Katrina had enough food to take on their escape.

"You'll do it. I stay here and check the maps for our route."

"Sounds like a good plan," Katrina said and put the picture frame inside the shawl-backpack.

"We'll leave in the morning," he said and gave her one last kiss, before she left the room in her quest to organize food for them.

Richard scrutinized the atlas. The scale was too big to glean directions, but at least he had an idea about distances and geography. One hundred miles westward to Görlitz, the border town into the Russian occupied sector of Germany, and from there another one hundred thirty miles northwest to Berlin. He had no idea how his home country looked after the devastating war, but he hoped to be able to catch a train or bus to Berlin. Surely, there was some transport available.

Unfortunately, he'd lost his German papers in the ruins of Mrs. Jaworski's farm, but that he'd take care of later. Half of the fugitives taking to the trek probably didn't have proper identification.

A bookworm all his life, he stuck his nose into the atlas, imagining the places to visit and the adventures to experience. Time passed in a whirlwind and when the clock on the mantelpiece struck noon, he reluctantly closed the atlas. It lay heavy in his hand. Too heavy to take with them.

His mind protested as his fingers opened up the correct page and began to tear out the sheets. But it had to be done. They needed every bit of information they could get. He neatly folded the sheets of paper and put them in his shirt pocket.

"Sorry for that," he whispered and put the majestic book back onto its place on the shelf. Then he roamed the kitchen to find things they'd need on the road.

Afterward, he sat and waited for Katrina to return.

In the evening the Adamskis returned, to find Katrina and Richard packing.

"So you're really leaving?" Barbara said.

"Yes, tomorrow before dawn," Richard answered.

"Tomorrow morning? So soon," Barbara said, with sorrow in her voice. But she didn't try to persuade Katrina to stay, for which Katrina was grateful.

After the trip to the black market earlier today and the awful atrocities she'd seen as the mob chased everything German, she increasingly feared not only for Richard, but also for her own life.

"It's in everyone's best interests. We're only a liability for you, if Ryszard is found out..." She couldn't finish the sentence. Didn't want to imagine what might happen despite their best efforts.

"Katrina, I'm sorry about yesterday. I know I won't be able to change your mind, but I don't want us to separate in anger," Barbara said, and Edmund nodded to reinforce the words of his wife.

"I'm not leaving with a row. I'm very grateful that you sheltered us for a while and if circumstances permit, I'll return in a year or less."

Richard cleared his throat. "Me, too, I'm very thankful for your help. It's not natural to receive someone from an enemy nation and extend kindness to them. As Katrina said, we'll visit as soon as the situation permits it."

"Godspeed," Barbara said and gave Katrina a hug.

Edmund extended his hand to shake Richard's hand, but loud knocks on the door made everyone stop and gaze out the window onto the street. A group of people lingered on the battered pavement and they heard angry voices while the hammering continued.

"I'll get it," Edmund said. But as soon as he opened the door into the hallway, the visitors stormed inside, shouting, "Where is he? Where's the German pig?"

Katrina's heart froze as she looked at Richard and watched the color fade from his face. "How...?" She glanced at her relatives, who wore identical expressions of shock and fear. "Did you...?"

"We didn't tell. How could you even suggest...?" Barbara cried, hurt and desperation etched on her face.

Three angry men pushed Edmund aside and stomped into the room. Katrina heard a door upstairs click shut. *So it must have been them. Someone in this house overheard our arguing last night and alerted the mob.* But she didn't have time to ponder her thoughts, because one of the men pushed her aside with such force she stumbled and fell against the coffee table.

The mob leader stood, scanning the room. His eyes paused on Edmund for a moment, and then landed upon Richard. "There he is!"

"I'm a Pole," Richard said and withdrew his forged papers from his shirt pocket. Only Katrina noticed the slightest tremble in his voice. The men didn't give them more than a casual glance.

"Anyone can have fake papers," the mob leader said, spitting on the floor. "I know a Nazi swine when I see one. And *you* are one."

"No! He's my cousin!" Katrina cried out, but before she finished her sentence, she felt Barbara's hand pressing over her mouth and the words came out but a muffled murmur.

"Shush. Or they will take you, too," Barbara whispered into her ear.

With Barbara closing her mouth and Edmund stepping in front of her, she had to helplessly watch two of the men each grab one of Richard's arms and drag him outside, forcing him down the street. She couldn't see more than a crowd, but she heard the vile name-calling directed at Richard and several other Germans.

Edmund closed the door and turned to look at Katrina, who wept angrily. "Where are they taking him? I have to find him!"

"There's nothing we can do for him. We can just be grateful they didn't take us as well.

CHAPTER 9

Richard's heart shattered as the brutes manhandled him down the street. Out of his peripheral vision, he observed the house where he'd lived, and registered with relief that nobody else followed him outside. The door was closed.

Katrina was safe. As were Barbara and Edmund.

For now.

He'd feared this day, and while he was resigned to his own fate, the look of profound sorrow on Katrina's face stabbed deep into his soul.

"Move it," a harsh voice said. Something hard shoved him in the back, causing him to fall to his knees as he lost his balance. Before he could get up, a booted foot landed in his side, forcing the air from his lungs. "Get up, pig."

Richard struggled to regain his footing under the incessant onslaught of kicks and strikes. He clenched his teeth to keep from screaming with pain and finally managed to get upright. The assault stopped as his attacker turned his attention to another man, who'd stumbled to the ground.

The group of German captives grew bigger as they were forced through the main street of Wroclaw, their captors generously doling out punches and whip lashes. The sidewalks filled with onlookers, cheering on the mob. A group of Russian soldiers stood at the market square. One of the soldiers pointed at the tumult and his comrades turned around. Richard hoped they'd intervene, but that sliver of hope evaporated when one of the soldiers flipped a cigarette stub to the ground and turned his head away.

In that heart-stopping moment, Richard realized he'd be lucky to survive this day.

"Stop!" someone shouted and the group came to a halt. Apparently at random, six of the German captives were picked out and led away. Richard's eyes widened in horror as he saw their destination. Screaming and kicking, each one of them received a noose around their neck, only to be hauled up to the lamppost lining the market square.

He closed his eyes, but his imagination filled in the images he didn't see, and bile rose in his throat. Soon enough the rest of the group was forced on, until they arrived at a fenced-in field.

Bruised, bloodied and hurting, Richard dropped to the ground, convinced that his last hour had struck. Something warm ran down his cheek and he touched his face, his finger red from his own blood. Too battered to do anything else, Richard collapsed in the dirt. He lay there, hoping for a quick end to his torment.

But luck wasn't on his side.

He must have passed out and slept through the night,

because a commotion woke him in the wee hours of the morning. Lying in the dirt, stiff from the chilly night and sleeping on the bare ground, he turned his head to see the commotion.

The mob came and delivered new prisoners, each of them a bloodied mess, and left them to their fate. But he soon concluded that was actually a blessing. Throughout the day the Poles came several times to retrieve a group of prisoners, dragging them away, beating, kicking and punching the unfortunate souls. Those who were taken never came back.

Richard would hear their agonizing screams and then nothing. Sometimes he heard a shot. The result was the same.

Deadly silence.

He shuddered. *What have we come to? The war is over, but another is just beginning. We humans are worse than wild animals.* He couldn't really blame the Poles for their thirst for revenge. They'd suffered under German oppression for six long years. Not for the first time, Richard was disgusted to be a German. Although he hadn't personally participated in the ferocious crimes, what had he done to stop it? What had the German people as a collective group done to stop it?

Nothing.

So how could he hope for mercy and leniency now?

Yet, he did. He hoped, wished and prayed this killing spree would end. That he could realize a future that included freedom. And plentiful food. And peace of mind.

And Katrina.

The morning moved into afternoon and the sun beat

down upon the wounded, replacing the agonizing pain with maddening, insupportable thirst. With every passing minute dehydration and the sense of desperation trickled deeper into Richard's being.

The only thing that kept him from drowning in misery was the knowledge of Katrina's safety. She was much better off without him. Barbara and Edmund would take good care of her, he was sure of that.

More and more prisoners arrived at the field. He gathered all his strength to crawl to the farthest corner from the entrance, figuring he'd be safest there from being taken away. By now, he'd concluded that leaving this camp meant certain death. It took the better part of an hour to struggle to his new hiding place. Every movement, every breath resulted in excruciating pain, from the bruises forming on his skin and probably several broken ribs.

Usually, the Poles chose apparently at random from the prisoners nearest to the entrance to take them to their "just punishment". The men were beaten to death, but the women awaited a different fate. One that became abundantly clear in the lecherous remarks of the guards.

Richard's mind flashed back to his time with the Wehrmacht in Lodz. The raid on Baluty together with the SS troops. Back then it had been the Polish women who'd suffered this age-old way to break not only the women, but also their men who couldn't protect them. He shuddered.

That day, he'd met Katrina. At least one beautiful thing had come from all the pain and suffering. A small smile stretched across his dry lips, cracking them. Even if he died today, the fates had blessed him with the most wonderful fifteen months with her.

When the night hit the land, he rolled into a ball, and tried to sleep. But the hunger pangs in his stomach, the unquenchable thirst and his constant worry about what the morrow would bring kept him awake until dawn broke again.

CHAPTER 10

"Don't! Wait!" Katrina screamed and shot up from the couch, her eyes getting used to the dim twilight at dawn. She fell back, angry sobs shaking her body.

"Are you alright?" Barbara left her bed to walk over and look after Katrina.

"I'm not! How can I ever be alright again? They've taken what I love most!" Katrina spat out, wanting to slam her fist against something hard.

"You need to calm down, or you'll endanger all of us." Edmund hovered over her. "Nobody is to know that you feel sympathy for a German."

Katrina couldn't help but glare daggers at him, although she knew he meant well. They had to ensure their own survival.

"I'll make tea," Barbara offered and hurried into the communal kitchen.

Katrina got up and dressed, her thoughts going in circles, trying to come up with a way to rescue Richard. She had to do something. Anything. She couldn't just let him die alone.

When she entered the kitchen, the two families from upstairs sat at the table, giving her a suspicious glance.

"I sure hope they teach those German pigs we don't want them here," one man said with a calculating grin.

"We're as shocked as anyone," Edmund quickly said. "He had all of us convinced he was a distant cousin from up North, one we hadn't seen since he was a baby."

The man sneered, apparently only half-believing, but not wanting to openly fight with fellow Poles. "He'll wish he could cross hell barefoot, when he finds out what we have in store for him."

Katrina's stomach squeezed and she felt the blood rushing from her face. In an effort not to give away her turmoil, she stepped to the stove, taking the ladle from Barbara's hand and saying, "Let me help you."

Barbara gave her a knowing wink and wiped her hands with her apron, before she walked away to get the cups from their room.

"My Anton is a guard at the camp, he'll see that none of the pigs feel cozy there," a brunette woman said with a wicked smile. "Shooting is too easy. They have to suffer first. Long and slow. I've heard some of the men have perfected the art of inducing excruciating pain for days without killing the victim."

Katrina couldn't believe her ears. How could this woman say something so cruel? How could she wish torture upon a fellow human being? Driven by pure rage she flew forward, grabbed the woman by the hair and screamed, "It was you! You betrayed him, you ugly bitch!"

"Bitch? You're the bitch here. German whore. If I were you, I'd be careful, or you'll soon be reunited with the bastards you love so much," the brunette yelled, defending herself against Katrina's attack.

In a whirlwind of scratching, biting and kicking, the two women formed a tangle of limbs. Katrina couldn't see or hear anything apart from the red in front of her eyes and the rushing in her ears. An overwhelming need to knock the smug grin of inhumanity right off that woman's face drove her forward with all her strength.

Suddenly she felt herself gripped by two big hands, tearing her away from the other woman. Half in the air, she continued to kick her feet until she heard Edmund's stern voice. "Calm down. Now."

With his fingers digging deep into the flesh of her shoulders while his other arm confined her at the waist, there wasn't much she could do. She went limp as Edmund carried her out of the kitchen and into their private room. After settling on the sofa, still shaking with fury, Katrina murmured, "I'm sorry for losing my temper."

"I'm afraid being sorry is not enough." Edmund said, as an exasperated Barbara rushed into the room, locking the door behind her and gazing at them with a mixture of sorrow and trepidation. "That woman will seek revenge. I'm almost certain she'll call the cops to come for you."

Katrina swallowed hard. How could she have let her emotions get the better of her? She should have known that attacking an informer would have consequences.

"What shall I do?" she asked with a feeble voice.

"Leave this house. Now," Edmund said.

"You can't kick her out onto the street," Barbara objected.

"It's not safe for you here anymore. The faster you leave, the greater your chances at survival."

"I'm..." Katrina had no idea what to say. Because he was right. When the cops arrived, they'd take her to the same camp they'd taken Richard.

Barbara only shook her head in sorrow. Again, it was Edmund who raised his voice, "Gather your things and leave through the back door. Now!"

With a dejected nod, Katrina rose from the sofa to stuff all of her and Richard's things into the rucksack she'd organized the day before. Her heart ached. If not for the betrayal of that woman, she and Richard would already be on their way to Berlin.

Katrina had never hated someone so much in her life.

In complete turmoil, she had no idea what to do next or where to go. Without him, it didn't make sense to embark on the dangerous trek, but neither could she stay in Wroclaw. She shouldered the rucksack and grimaced at the heavy weight of the food she'd bartered for the silver frame.

For a moment, she hesitated. Should she leave half of it with Barbara and Edmund? Despite their dislike for the Nazis, they'd sheltered Richard in their home, exposing themselves to danger.

But then she scolded herself. *Have you already given up on him? Good partner you are!* A newfound determination flushed her body and she straightened her shoulders. She would find Richard and rescue him, so help her God.

Barbara stood and watched her, a very solemn expression on her face.

"Thank you for everything," Katrina said and gave her a hug.

"Godspeed, my child. Let us know when you're safe." Barbara pressed a few ruble notes into her hand. "It's not much, but it will help. Now go to the back door; Edmund is waiting for you."

The kindness and generosity of her mother's cousin brought tears to Katrina's eyes and she blinked them away. Unable to speak, she only nodded her head and gave Barbara another hug – not knowing whether she'd ever see her again.

Katrina peered out of their room into the empty hallway and then tiptoed to the back door. It wouldn't do to alert the vile neighbors of her escape. She opened the door slowly and scanned the small garden until she saw the gate leading to a path between the houses. The rusty metal hung ajar and since she didn't see Edmund anywhere, she crossed the garden in some haste and slunk out through the gate.

"Shush," a voice whispered. When she turned she saw a big man standing half-covered by the hedge. He waved her over and she recognized Edmund, holding something.

"This will help you get around easier." He stepped aside and revealed an old black bicycle leaning against the hedge.

"I can't possibly accept this," Katrina protested.

"You can and you will. Listen, I know you're planning to rescue your boyfriend. I think it's a suicide mission and absolutely irresponsible. And while I don't approve of it, I would probably attempt the same if I were still your age."

Katrina's jaw fell. Edmund usually didn't talk that much, and she'd always had the feeling that he'd never completely approved of his wife's taking Katrina and Richard into their home.

Edmund didn't wait for her to say anything and continued, "They are taking the Germans to the former football field right outside the city walls. You know where that is?"

Katrina nodded.

"Not all of the Poles agree with the brutalities committed, and there's one guard, he used to be a friend of mine long before the war. We don't talk much these days, but despite everything I know he has a good heart. He might be able to help."

"Do you really think he will help me to free Richard?" Katrina asked with a pounding heart, the glimmer of hope taking possession of her soul.

"I can't guarantee it, but he's your best chance – maybe your only one."

"How do I recognize him?"

"His name is Jozef and he's lost his left arm."

"Thank you. And I'm sorry if we caused you problems." Katrina gave him a handshake.

"Don't worry about us. I have some connections to the new city administration. Nothing will happen to us. Now, go."

Katrina climbed onto the bicycle. It was a big, black monster of iron and she had to stretch her toes to reach the pedals. But Edmund was right, they'd be much faster pedaling than walking. Now she only had to find the guard, get to Richard, free him and escape to Germany.

She scoffed at the sheer impossibility of her undertaking, and hopelessness threatened to sweep away her determination. Gritting her teeth, she pedaled harder, leaving the dirt path behind and taking a turn onto the main street that would lead her to the football field.

And Richard.

I hope he's still there. Her heart froze in agony as she considered the possibility that he was already dead. *No. He can't be dead. Dear God, please, let Richard still be alive.*

CHAPTER 11

Richard let out a pained groan as he turned in his sleep. Jolted awake from the stabbing pain in his ribcage, he glanced around. It was deep into the night and only the half-moon cast the field in an eerie light.

Most of the prisoners had fallen into an exhausted sleep and nobody moved about. But the groans of pain mixed with snoring and soft weeping wouldn't let silence settle over the camp.

He'd spent many a night out in the open during his time on the Eastern front, but never, not even cowering in the trenches, had he felt the icy hand of death as oppressively as tonight. Dozens of prisoners wouldn't see the light of the morning as they tragically succumbed to the wounds inflicted by the ravaging Poles.

Even more would perish the next day at the hands of their torturers. He wondered what fate had in store for him. Would he be shot in the head? Tortured first? Or would he be sent to a forced labor camp to slave away his life in one of Poland's mines?

From what he'd heard, the Poles had taken a page from the Nazi book and continued to run the atrocious concentration camps – only switching the liberated inmates with new ones. If anything, they were even crueler than the former oppressor, as their goal wasn't simply to kill, but to inflict suffering first.

He dozed off again and woke at the sound of a bell at dawn.

"Wake up! Lazy sleazeballs!" a harsh voice shouted over a megaphone. "Everyone line up!"

Richard muttered a curse as he heaved up his aching bones and stepped in line with thousands of other prisoners, separated into males and females. He stood there, breathing shallowly so as not to hurt his ribs any more than he already had, and waited.

Left and right, men fell to the ground, unable to keep upright. The first time he witnessed it, Richard bent down to help the unfortunate soul up again. A rifle butt landed on his back and he let out a scream.

"Stand! Asshole!" a Polish guard commanded and Richard hurried to follow the orders. If he wanted to survive, he had to obey every order to the letter.

The minutes trickled away, and the sun crawled up the horizon, indicating another hot day. At night, he'd licked drops of dew from the fence, but even now in the early morning the maddening thirst raised its ugly head.

He must have been standing motionless for an hour or two, or maybe three, when a group of official-looking men entered the camp and started to ask every prisoner for name, birthdate and birthplace.

A ray of hope entered his anguished mind. Could he lie his way out of this camp? Pretend to be a Pole? He fingered the papers in his chest pocket. They were still there. Life insurance, or death sentence?

One of the officials seemed to be some kind of bureaucrat, while two of the others wore police uniforms and one a soldier's uniform. Richard had to look twice: the man in a soldier's uniform was missing one arm.

During the Russian campaign, he'd seen many of his comrades wounded and many with limbs torn from them. They were whisked away to the field hospitals and – if they survived the ordeal – discharged from the Wehrmacht and returned home.

Guilt seeped down his spine. He'd completely forgotten about those less fortunate than him and erased their fates from his memory. He'd spent the last year of the war quite comfortable on Mrs. Jaworski's farm, tilling the fields. Until today, he'd never given a thought about what awaited the injured after their return to civilian life. But of course, they must live on something and work at some kind of job.

The bureaucrat apparently was the boss and asked the questions, while the two policemen generously doled out knocks and slams with their rifle butts, if a prisoner didn't answer fast enough. The one-armed soldier, though, stood by and watched, his eye twitching whenever they would order a prisoner to step out of the line.

Then, one of two things happened: either the man was shot at point-blank range, sending a jolt of terror through every other captive in the camp, or he'd be shoved to a small area, to stand and wait. *Wait for what?* Richard mused, although he'd gleaned from the whispers around him that waiting might be as bad or worse than being shot dead. Usually the people who'd had a quarrel with the policemen in the past were the ones destined for *special treatment*.

Richard shrivelled to half his size when the group of men stopped in front of him.

"Name?"

"Ryszard Blach."

The leader raised an eyebrow. "Born?"

Berlin, he wanted to say, but caught himself and hesitated for a split-second, before he carefully pronounced the name of the town on his forged papers. "Chojnice."

"Chojnice, eh?" one of the policemen said with a sneer. "What does a German pig do up there?"

"I'm a Pole," Richard answered, hoping the men would believe him.

"A Pole?" The bureaucrat scrutinized him with small eyes. "I'm sure you have papers to prove this fact?"

Richard nodded and slowly raised his hands. One of the rifles twitched nervously in his direction and Richard waged an internal argument with himself whether he should explain and risk being found out by his accent, or stay silent and risk being shot on the spot.

He stopped moving his hands and said, "Papers are in my chest pocket."

"Don't move. We take them," the leader said and pointed to the soldier to get the papers.

Richard stared into the muzzles of two rifles trained at him, while the soldier stepped forward. He held his breath in an effort to stand absolutely still. The thin and unkempt man gave Richard a perfunctory search, before he reached for the papers in his chest pocket and handed them to his superior.

His breath smelled of alcohol and Richard recognized the bloodshot eyes of a habitual drinker. For a short moment he felt pity for this man, a former soldier like him, who'd lost a limb, his youth and his illusions and now resorted to the merciful befuddlement the alcohol provided. In another life, he surely had been a good, morally upright man.

It was a shame how this godawful war had crippled an entire generation of young men, mentally, physically and psychologically. Richard himself had seen enough to last for several lifetimes, but thanks to his ability to retreat into the world of the books he so loved, he'd managed to stay more or less sane.

"Ah, let's see," the superior said and gave a low whistle as he scrutinized the papers. "Ryszard Blach, born in Chojnice in April 1925. Now tell me, what are you doing in Wroclaw?"

There was no escape, and Richard knew it. The hard glint in the eyes of the interrogator reflected a hidden malice. A complacent smugness as if he had laid a trap and was now waiting for Richard to gnaw off his own leg trying to get out of it.

"Sir, my house was bombed and I came here to live with a cousin." The slight tremble in Richard's voice reverberated through his bones and he saw the lips of his opponent twitch.

"Visiting your cousin? You sure you're not a damn lying German pig?" The bureaucrat's hand shot out to hit Richard square in the face and he swayed from the impact. For a desk jockey this man had an amazing uppercut.

"I'm a Pole," Richard insisted.

"Well then, you won't have any difficulty speaking after me: *W Szczebrzeszynie chrząszcz brzmi w trzcinie, i Szczebrzeszyn z tego słynie, że chrząszcz brzmi tam w Szczebrzeszynie.*"

Richard's blood turned to ice. The maniacal man's words were a popular Polish tongue-twister and Katrina had always giggled at his hapless butchering of the language.

"*W Szczebrzesz...nie...brzi...*" Damn! Not even in the face of death could he force his tongue to pronounce the difficult words.

The man opposite him broke out in laughter. "So much for being a Pole. My two-year-old grandson can recite better than you." Then he held the papers high up and shredded them with a malicious smile, letting the small pieces of paper fall to the ground. "It's a shame, actually. One of the best sets of forged papers I've seen in a while. But still fake."

One of the policemen shoved the butt of his gun in Richard's stomach. He doubled over in pain and covered his head with his arms as more kicks rained down on his backside. He wondered if he'd improve his chances at survival by telling them that he was a Wehrmacht deserter and asking to be handed over to the Russians, or if he should keep quiet and pretend to be a civilian. Either way, his life had just entered a new sort of hell.

"Take him over there," the leader of the group yelled and seconds later, one big hand grabbed him and heaved him up, not too roughly, and pulled him to the separated *waiting area.*

Richard's heart sank as the man whom he recognized as the soldier dropped him onto the ground. He caught a glimpse of the soldier's eyes and believed he saw a trace of embarrassment in them. Again, Richard felt pity for him. This man wasn't cruel and sadistic like the two policemen, but he probably felt there was no choice for him but to do the ugly bidding tasked upon him.

Unable to move, with every excruciating breath, Richard lay still on the ground, fearing an unknown and terrifying future. Meanwhile, the roll call in the camp continued and every now and then another man stumbled into the waiting area, collapsing to the ground, as soon as the guards let go of him.

Bedazzled with pain, Richard retreated into his mind, finding a modicum of relief in the story of The Ingenious Nobleman Sir Don Quixote of La Mancha. It kept him alive, breathing, and his heart beating, disconnected from harsh reality.

A loud thud and a dull pain in his leg jolted him out of his fantasy and he raised his head. A man in priest's garb had fallen atop him. Richard sat up to shake the man off of him, but when he turned him around, his stomach turned. The man's face was hardly recognizable as a human being's.

He moved him as softly as he could and took off his jacket to put it under the man's head. Then he moved to sit behind him, to shield his face from the scorching sun that travelled across the horizon.

The priest seemed to be unconscious, murmuring unintelligible words and groaning in pain every now and then.

Richard bit on his lip to keep the outrage and anger at bay, hopelessness seeping into his bones.

When the guards arrived again with a new prisoner, Richard asked one of them, "Could I get some water for this priest, please?"

But the guard only laughed at him and left again.

"Son," the priest whispered, interrupted by coughs. "You should not worry for me, as I'll soon be with God. Pray for our captors, who have sinned."

Richard didn't think the vile Polish guards deserved his prayers, but he nodded so as not to upset the dying man.

"I can tell by your expression that you don't agree with me, but we need to bring love and forgiveness into this world riddled with hate and revenge. Remember, Jesus sacrificed himself to save humanity."

"You are right," Richard said, still not fully accepting the priest's gracious words. But he would bring some love into this world and stay with this man during his last hours on earth. So he moved over and held the priest's hand. After a while he started to talk. About his love for books, about life on the farm with Katrina and his fear of never seeing her again. He talked for hours and the priest smiled every now and then, but never uttered a word. Not until he suddenly became restless and tried to get up.

"Shush, easy," Richard said.

"No, no. My time has come, I have to..." The priest somehow managed to sit and removed a necklace with a golden cross from around his neck. "This is for you. May it help you through difficult times."

Richard was moved to tears and could only murmur a

soft "Thank you" as he took the valuable article and slipped it over his head.

"I have no regrets," the priest said and stopped breathing.

Richard had seen many people die. Enemy soldiers, comrades at the front, civilians shot in cold blood, his best friend Karl captured by the partisans, Mrs. Jaworski... it was an endless line. But the priest, now lying dead by his side, moved him to tears and he silently wept for everything that was cruel and awful and full of hate in this world.

He took back his jacket and sat silently waiting. But nothing happened. Seemingly the guards had forgotten about the men waiting to be taken for torture, and the night began to settle over the land.

CHAPTER 12

It took Katrina most of the day to locate the one-armed guard but she finally spotted him as he left the camp in the afternoon. She followed him to a shabby bar, where he sat down at the counter.

"Vodka. Make it double, and chalk it up on the slate," he said to the haggard waitress, who cast him a quick glance before she went to fetch the bottle.

"Here's your drink, Jozef," the waitress said as she put a smeared glass in front of him and generously poured the alcohol into the glass. He downed it in one gulp.

Katrina lingered near the door, unsure of herself. This had to be the man Edmund told her about, the man who could serve as Richard's savior. Although she had her doubts whether he'd be willing to help. A ruined man drowning his despair in vodka. She knew the kind.

"What do you want?" the waitress said with a nod to Katrina.

"Eh... I..."

"This is no place to loiter. Order something or leave."

Katrina's heart thundered against her ribs and she gathered all her courage to say, "Actually, I was looking for Jozef."

"Me?" Jozef turned around with a bewildered look on his face. His eyes became small slits as he gave her a once-over from head to toe. Panic trickled down her skin in the wake of his piercing stare. It transformed into an approving leer once he'd finished the perusal of her person.

"Yes, my cousin Edmund Adamski said you might be able to help," she said, trying her best to disguise the slight tremble in her voice.

"Hmm... Edmund... and what can I do for such a beautiful doll?"

By now several other patrons had raised their heads with interest and Katrina fought the urge to run from the bar. "Can we talk about this in private?" she asked with a feeble voice.

"In private? Of course." The lecherous glint in his eyes frightened her, but it was too late to back out. Jozef left his seat at the bar and came toward her. Grabbing her by the elbow, he led her into a back alley. There he released her, and she stumbled backward. The man fingered a cigarette from his pocket, put it into his mouth, and searched his pocket for a lighter, all the while she was standing frozen, staring at him.

After he lit it, he blew smoke into her face and asked, "Now, what do you want from me?"

"I'm looking for my fiancé." Another cloud of smoke hit her face and she scrunched her nose. "He's been taken to the camp."

"A German? I don't do Germans."

"He's a Pole, but was mistaken for a German," Katrina lied, hoping Richard's common sense had compelled him to stick to their cover story.

"Must be an epidemic."

Katrina stared round-eyed at the crazy man and when he didn't offer any further explanation she added, "His name is Ryszard Blach."

Jozef guffawed. "That lad. Not sure whether he's still alive. They left him in pretty bad shape after tearing his false papers to pieces."

"You've seen him?" Katrina whispered, fighting against the dizziness unsteadying her stance.

"Yep. Personally put him into the waiting area." He put the stub into the corner of his mouth and raised his arm to scratch his badly shaven chin. "Not a nice sight. But kinda tough, the lad. Wouldn't whine and whimper or beg." He cocked his head. "I'm sure he's a deserter. Know a soldier when I see one."

"Please, can you help me get him out of the camp?" Katrina didn't actually believe anymore that this unsavory man in his threadbare uniform might help her, but she had to pursue every possibility.

"I may. But you'll have to pay."

"Pay? How much?" The blood drained from her face. She possessed nothing but the well-hidden bicycle and the few personal belongings and food she carried in the rucksack.

Jozef licked his lips and mentioned an extortionate amount of money.

"I don't have that amount of money, but I have a bicycle," she said. Without the bicycle the escape would become so much more tedious, but she'd rather give it up and have Richard by her side.

"I don't need no bicycle. Can't even ride it with only one arm. Sell it and come back with the money tomorrow. Although your man might not be alive by then. My best guess is they'll take him to the torture hall in the morning." Katrina had difficulties interpreting his confusing expression. He seemed to be ashamed, sad even, but also excited and... aroused. A sense of danger curled her toes.

"Won't you find the kindness to help me save his life?" she asked in desperation.

"Why should I? Did any of the German bastards help me when I was wounded?" He spat the glowing stub to the ground and eyed her with unconcealed lust. Then he grinned, exposing two gaps in his teeth, and said, "You could offer me yourself."

Katrina took a step backward in shock. "I couldn't."

"Then we have nothing left to discuss." He turned around and walked away, leaving Katrina completely gutted, desolation her only companion as the walls of the alley seemed to close in on her. She wanted to scream with desperation. Could she survive with her beloved one's death on her conscience, just because she wasn't willing to sacrifice her honor in exchange for his freedom?

"Wait!" she yelled after Jozef. Deep in her heart she knew she'd never forgive herself if she didn't do everything in her power to save Richard's life. Thinking about sleeping with the repulsive guard made her want to vomit, but she'd survive. And Richard, too.

"Changed your mind?"

"I'll do it. I'll sleep with you."

His face lit up and she almost panicked. A frightening thought entered her mind. What if she made this sacrifice and then this man wouldn't stick to his end of the bargain? Or Richard was already dead?

"But first you'll get Richard out of the camp."

His face fell, but after a few moments a crooked smile appeared on his lips. "Not only pretty, but also brave. And intelligent. You have a deal. Meet me in front of the camp in two hours from now."

"In two hours?" Katrina repeated, somewhat dumb-founded.

"Yes. Don't look so surprised. It'll get dark soon and these things are best done under cover of night." He turned on his heel and walked away.

CHAPTER 13

A soft foot kick penetrated Richard's dreams and he instinctively huddled into a ball. Another kick followed, accompanied by a hushed command, "Wake up."

He couldn't believe he'd dozed off with the priest's cold, lifeless corpse snuggled up against him. Even worse, no one cared. Some poor sap would be forced to collect the dead in the morning and dump them in a mass grave as if they meant nothing.

After this newest jolt of agony, he forced his eyes open and glanced up to see the one-armed soldier who'd dumped him here the day before, pointing directly at him. "Hurry up. I don't have all night."

Richard pushed himself to his feet, swallowing down the groans of pain, convinced he'd be led like a lamb to his slaughter.

"Come with me. Quick."

"Where are you taking me?"

The guard didn't answer, and his demeanor made it clear

that Richard was not to ask any further questions. So he simply walked beside the man through the sleeping camp. The peculiar situation considerably heightened his blood pressure. Usually the captors didn't bother the prisoners at night. What could possibly be so important they had to interrogate him in the middle of night?

This must be a bad sign.

The stench of death hung heavy in the air and mist rose from the damp, dew-covered ground. Richard yearned to lick some of the drops from the few remaining blades of grass to quench his thirst.

He and Katrina had been hungry before, but never thirsty. Not like this. His body had long ago stopped producing saliva and his tongue stuck to his palate. Stench and dust accumulated in his nostrils and his mouth, and every swallow was only a dry contraction of sore muscles.

"Wait!" the guard grunted.

Richard stopped, staying motionless until the guard waved him over into the shadow of a tree. Something was seriously wrong here. Did the guard want to settle a score? But why? They had never met before. Or had they and Richard had simply forgotten? Or was the guard mistaking him for another man?

As his head throbbed in protest, he stilled his thoughts. It didn't help to worry; he'd rather focus and be alert for whatever came. Harboring the hope of escape, his subconscious suddenly conjured up a tiny person at the other side of the fence, who looked a lot like Katrina. He was starting to hallucinate. That was a widely known side effect from dehydration, so he did his best to banish the image from his mind and continued to wait.

The guard discussed something with that person and then returned. "Come with me, you're free to go."

"Free? Why? What?" Richard's brain was slow and viscous like honey.

"Come."

On the other side of the fence, joy overwhelmed Richard when his hallucinatory angel started to move toward him. She rushed over to wrap her arms around him and he almost fell to his knees at the sudden turn of events.

But the joy didn't last long, because the guard stepped between them and said, "First my payment."

Despite the darkness of the night, Richard saw her ashen face lined with a tragic expression. The distress oozing off of her stabbed him in the stomach. A terrible suspicion popped into his mind and he recoiled from the impact. It wasn't far-fetched to imagine what kind of payment a beautiful, but otherwise destitute, woman could offer to a man like the guard.

"You?" he whispered to her.

"I had to. It was the only way." Her eyes filled with anguish and he wished he could do something to stop this madness. Anything.

"We can do it behind the shack over there." The guard grabbed Katrina's elbow with his one hand and started to lead her away.

"Wait," Richard hissed, his heart broken over the sacrifice she was prepared to make.

For him.

The guard turned his head with an annoyed expression, "That was the deal. You'd better disappear or you'll get caught again."

Richard raised his hand to his hurting heart and felt a strange object hanging from his neck. The golden cross. The priest certainly had meant a more spiritual assistance when he'd endowed him the cross to guide him through difficult times. But he wasn't in a situation to pick and chose.

"I will pay you," he pressed out.

"You? I searched you yesterday, remember? You have nothing of value," the guard said.

"I have this." Richard took the necklace from his neck and held it up. The golden cross caught a ray of moonlight and reflected a golden shine onto the face of the guard. His craggy face lit up at the sight.

"Well, now this," the guard let go of Katrina's elbow and stepped toward Richard, "now this beauty is even better than her. It'll pay for all my debts and then some." He smiled and took the necklace from Richard's hands. "Good luck, you'll need it," he said and disappeared into the darkness.

Katrina launched herself into Richard's arms, but only for a few short seconds. Once she escaped his embrace again, she said, "Hurry. We have to get out of Wroclaw."

"I know."

Katrina grabbed his hand and pulled him after her. Now that the surge of adrenaline had left his body, the throbbing aches returned, and the debilitating thirst.

"Water. I need water," he croaked.

Katrina didn't slow down but fumbled through the rucksack he hadn't noticed before and handed him a bottle of water. He drank the entire contents in one long, refreshing, resuscitating gulp and stored the bottle in her rucksack again.

"We'll have to refill it somewhere," she said and kept pulling him after her.

"Where are we going?"

"To Berlin."

Shockwaves of agony rushed through his mistreated bones. He doubted that he'd withstand a two-hundred-fifty-mile walk in his current condition.

Katrina stopped at a pile of rubble and ducked behind it, leaving him wondering what on earth she was doing. A minute later he saw and a broad grin spread across his face.

"Good woman, you have no idea how much I love you," he said and pressed a kiss on her lips.

"You love me or my worldly possessions?" she giggled once he let go of her lips.

"I love both. But most of all I love you for what you were willing to sacrifice for me."

Her face took on an embarrassed flush and she averted her eyes. "We should hurry."

Richard took the bicycle from her hands and positioned himself on the saddle, his feet steady on the ground at both sides. "Hop on the crossbar and hold tight."

She perched on the crossbar, the rucksack on her back touching his arm, and he started to pedal. "Where to?"

"Follow this road to the end and then turn left. We'll take the longer route outside the city perimeter instead of crossing through."

"Wise decision."

They didn't talk much, apart from the occasional directions on where to go, because he had to focus on keeping the bicycle steady with her additional weight. The city still lay in darkness and the roads were bad. Many a time they almost toppled over, but somehow, he managed to keep them upright.

He pedaled mile after mile, fleeing from the place that had almost become his final resting place. He pedaled on, even when his strength began to wane and the pain in his body screamed at him to stop and rest.

He pedaled.

And pedaled.

And pedaled.

Defying his own body that demanded him to stop. The burning sensation in his calves, the dull pain in his ribs at every inhalation. The excruciating agony whenever the bicycle hit a bump in the road. The pins and needles in his hands, that turned into numbness.

He even defied the hunger pains and the return of his thirst, because of his singular focus on getting them as far away from Wroclaw as possible. He knew he wouldn't be able to make the entire journey to Görlitz in one day, but he vowed not to stop before they were in a comparatively safe place.

CHAPTER 14

Hours passed, and every muscle in Katrina's body ached from perching on the crossbar. The rough surface of the road gave her bones a good shaking. She had long ago lost the feeling in her bum, and her upper legs burned from the effort of keeping them out of the way of Richard's knees, which rhythmically went up and down.

The rucksack weighed heavily on her shoulders, but she held her tongue, resisting the temptation to ask Richard for a break. He must be hurting even more, since he was doing all the hard work, while she merely had to keep her balance on the hard pole.

They had decided to follow the winding road along the Oder until the river turned north. It was still a while to go, but they needed to cross the Oder to get to Görlitz, the southernmost town on the new border between Poland and Germany.

She turned her head slightly to catch a glimpse of his face. His usually attractive visage was distorted into a grim expression of determination and pain. His blond hair was matted and dirty, as was his unkempt stubble. Encrusted blood adorned his brow, cheek and lip. But to her he was still the most handsome man in the world. She longed to reach out her hand and caress his skin, but giggled at the thought, because the movement would only serve to upset their fragile balance and send them both tumbling to the ground.

"What's so funny?" Richard asked through gritted teeth.

"Nothing. I giggled, because our situation really can't get much worse." They continued to ride in silence. Once in a while they passed other refugees walking the same road in their quest to reach the safety of Germany.

When Richard's huffing and puffing became increasingly labored, she said, "Stop over there, you need a break."

"Can't… need to get away…"

"Richard, you're no use to me when you collapse on the bicycle. See that patch of trees? We'll rest right there."

He didn't protest any further and brought the vehicle to a halt. Katrina slid down from the crossbar with a sigh of relief, the soreness in her buttocks and upper thighs making her eyes water with pain. She discarded the rucksack and stretched her aching bones. When she turned around, she saw the bicycle and her man lying side by side in the grass beneath the trees. Richard's eyes were closed, and his face showed a heated red color.

The cold hand of fear squeezed the breath from her lungs and she launched herself at him, ready to wake him from the dead. "Darling, please, are you alive?"

"Yes. Need water," came his coarse reply and she took

the bottle from the rucksack, opening it, before she remembered it was empty.

"You stay right here, I'll go and get water from the river." Drinking the Oder water wasn't ideal, not when upstream in Wroclaw the corpses were piled up in the water, but she didn't have another choice.

She hurried across the empty road and climbed the muddy bank down to the river, where she glanced at the water, making sure there weren't any rotting cadavers nearby. Then she filled the bottle and drank it in one gulp, before she refilled it and attempted to climb up the bank again.

"Shoot," she cursed as she slid down the slippery slope, delaying her from bringing back the precious liquid to her boyfriend. She should have taken the rucksack, because with the bottle in one hand she couldn't pull herself up along the slope. A second attempt brought the same results. The loamy earth was too slippery. She'd need both of her hands to crawl up.

She stood and looked for a better place, but the bank was covered with mud and slick grass. Finally, she stuffed the bottle into her blouse and crawled up to the road. When she reached it and stood up, she looked down at her mud-caked skirt. Just a minor inconvenience in a string of major disasters.

She swiped her hands and shoes in the grass, fumbled the bottle from her blouse and hurried back to her boyfriend, who lay in the grass exactly the same way she'd left him.

"Here you go."

Richard opened his eyes and sat up with some trouble.

Then he emptied the bottle and handed it back to her. "Can I have some more, please?"

"I'll bring more," she said, reluctant to make the journey a second time. But whether she liked it or not, they needed more water. "Can you cut some of the bread and a bit of the ham for us? We have plenty of food, but we still need to ration it, because we don't know how long we'll be on the road."

He nodded and reached for the backpack, while Katrina trotted off to the river. She eyed the dreadful mud bank and walked down the road, hoping to find a better place. About five minutes further along she saw a sandy patch in the river that might have been used as a passage. She followed a trail covered in pebbles down to the water and came to stand upon a small pebble beach.

The scenery would have been beautiful, if it weren't for the destroyed remains of a bridge leading across the river. She took off her shoes and socks, gathered up her skirt and dipped her toes into the water. It was refreshing but not too cold. Maybe they could use the ford to cross over to the other bank. A few steps into the stream she was just over her knees in the water. During her next step, a strong current tugged at her leg and her foot stepped into the void. She stood one-legged with flailing arms, trying to regain her balance.

"Hey, lady, get out of there," someone shouted at her and she saw an old man rushing over to grab her hand. Once she was safely at the shore again, she wondered where he'd suddenly come from.

"Thank you for your help," she said.

"What you doing here?"

"Looking for a way to cross. I thought this might be a passage."

"It was. But not since they destroyed the bridge. The detonation took out a piece of the riverbed and caused a treacherous undercurrent. No way to cross this time of the year. Maybe in summer."

"You live nearby?" she asked.

The old man smiled, exposing a row of crooked, blackened teeth. "About ten miles from here. I come here because the fishing is still good."

"Is there another bridge intact?"

"Don't think so. But there's a ferry a few days' walk downstream. At least there was last week. But with all the bloody Germans running for their lives, who knows?" He spat on the ground.

"Thank you for your help. I'll be on my way." Katrina thought it prudent not to mention that she was travelling with one of those bloody Germans. The old man gave her a last glance before he trotted off around a bend to resume his fishing.

Katrina put on her shoes, tied the laces and then set off to bring Richard the water. As she approached the group of trees, she saw him leaning against a trunk, two slices of bread and two slices of ham lying neatly on a piece of cloth.

She smiled, remembering her youth. On Sundays, her parents would sometimes take the four children and go on a picnic with them. She had loved the carefree hours filled with her mother's delicious food, laughter and endless play. A sigh escaped her. Those times were gone – for good.

But she hoped that one day, she and Richard would have children of their own, and the future would allow for a happy family far from the horrors of war. The war was over, but everywhere she looked, devastation prevailed, and living conditions had become worse instead of better.

Richard and she were caught in some special kind of hell, where they neither belonged, nor were safe, with one side or the other. She just hoped this would all get better once they reached Germany.

"Here's more water," she said, holding the bottle high in her hand, surprised at the look of horror in Richard's eyes.

"What on earth has happened to you?"

"Nothing. I…" She looked down at her clothing, which was caked in mud from her first trip to the river, the hem of her skirt dripping with water from her near-encounter with having to swim. That he hadn't noticed before showed how exhausted he'd been. "That happened when I had to crawl up the mud bank from the river on my first trip to get water."

He cast her a sheepish grin. "Must have evaded my perception."

She laughed out loud, and collapsed onto the grass beside him. Snorting, she said, "You crack me up. I have no idea how you could even keep the bicycle moving in your condition. The moment we stopped, you plummeted to the ground."

"It's called the law of inertia. It was easier to keep going than changing my state of motion." He cast her one of those full-on grins she loved so much, and she pressed a kiss on his chapped lips before she answered.

"I had no idea you devoured physics books with the same speed you read literature."

"Back in school, I loved physics and chemistry almost as

much as German literature." He sighed heavily. "I do miss books. A lot."

Katrina took a piece of bread and said, "I considered taking one of the books from the house when I left Barbara and Edmund."

He looked at her with so much love in his eyes, she almost melted into a puddle. Then he took her hand and said, "Thanks for considering it. But I'm glad you had the good sense not to do so. It wouldn't go over well if someone found a German book on us when we're pretending to be Poles."

"Are we still pretending to be Poles?"

He sighed again, a glint of fear taking up residence in his eyes. "They tore my papers to pieces, so I'm now officially an undocumented alien."

"Without the papers to support the ruse there's no chance anybody will believe your cover story."

"Once we are across the new border, we won't need the ruse anymore. But the problem is..." Richard said, finishing off his slice of ham. He wiped his mouth, smearing more dirt on his face in the process, and then took a gulp from the bottle.

"... crossing the border," Katrina completed his sentence. "I don't think being paperless will pose a problem. There must be thousands of refugees who've lost their papers."

"Yes, but..." His bright blue eyes bored holes into her and she physically felt his anxiety.

She said, "None of the other refugees is a twenty-year-old Wehrmacht deserter. We need to find an excuse why you weren't drafted."

"I don't want to fall into Russian hands. From what I've

heard it's similar to my experience in the camp in Wroclaw."
He shuddered as he spoke.

Katrina laid a hand on his, worried by the trace of defeat
in his stare. The days in the camp must have been a horrific
experience, and while she was glad to have him with her,
she also worried about his condition. His bruised and
battered face left her in fear about the rest of his body.

"I met an old man when I fetched water at the river. He
told me there's a ferry across the Oder a few days' walk
downstream. We should try to get there."

"I agree. The faster we cross the border, the better."

"Why don't we pack up, and I'll show you the gravel path
down to the river so we can wash up, drink, and refill our
bottle. Then we're our way in a jiffy."

Richard shouldered the rucksack and let out a short
scream, but stubbornly refused to let her carry the bag.
Katrina grabbed the bicycle and walked beside him, the bike
rolling along between them until they reached the gravel
path. She already feared the journey perched on the
crossbar again, but it would have to be. They were traveling
so much faster like this.

She took the bicycle with them down to the bank, always
afraid someone might steal their only means of transport.
When Richard took off his jacket and shirt to wash in the
stream, she heard a ripping sound and a muttered curse. She
looked up at him and gasped in horror. His back was full of
seeping wounds, torn open by ripping off the encrusted
cloth, and there were deep black bruises scattered across his
ribs.

"Wait, let me," she said and washed his shirt in the cool
water, before she wrung it out and started to carefully clean

his wounds. "I'm in awe that you could even pedal like this. You must have broken a few ribs as well."

"I'm sure I did." He tried a crooked grin, gritting his teeth when the damp cloth touched his skin. "It hurts with every breath."

"Once we reach the ferry, I'll be on the lookout for some medicinal herbs to help the healing."

"You and your herbs," he said with a teasing smile.

"Don't mess with me or I'll make you eat a handful of fennel seeds."

Richard hated anything fennel and as she had intended, he made a disgusted face and protested, "No need to be cruel, I promise to behave."

She finished cleaning his wounds and washed his shirt again, while he filled the bottle and poured it over his head, thus meagerly washing his hair and face.

"Much better," she said as she handed him the considerably cleaner wrung-out shirt. "With the sunshine and the airflow it'll dry in no time at all."

Richard got dressed again and then stared at her, mischief twinkling in his eyes. "Aren't you going to wash up, little mud pie?"

"What, here?"

"There's nobody around."

Katrina glanced suspiciously up and down the bank, and then back at Richard. "Someone could be walking down the road."

"Nobody will come. If it'll ease your mind, I'll watch." He said it with such a dirty smile that she felt her entire body flush with heat.

"No you won't. You'll turn around and watch the road."

She had to bite back a giggle at his disappointed face. Although she missed being intimate with him, it wouldn't happen here, out in the open for everyone to see who happened to pass by.

When he dutifully turned around, she peeked around the bend in the river to make sure the old man was gone and then took off her blouse to wash her face, arms, and chest, before she washed and wrung out the blouse to put it back on. Only then did she call out to Richard, "Anyone in sight?"

He turned around, raising a brow at the sight of her wet blouse. "Nobody but the most beautiful woman on earth, and I missed the best part."

"You keep watching out," she answered and then slipped out of her skirt to wash off the mud. In a short while she told him, "Finished."

"See, nobody passed by, and I could have helped you lather your back."

Katrina giggled. "We don't have soap to lather."

"I could have used my bare hands to do the task."

"You keep those thoughts to yourself – we have some cycling to do."

CHAPTER 15

Richard took the bicycle from her hands and started pedaling as soon as she'd climbed back atop the crossbar. He felt slightly better after some food and rest, but his muscles were sore, and his ribs hurt. Nevertheless, he was determined to hold up until they reached the ferry.

The road was narrow and winding, and in better times he would have called it picturesque. Today, though, he had no time to watch what remained of the beautiful landscape, because he had to keep his eyes peeled on the road, furrowed by deep creases caused by heavy Panzers. He'd seen before how German and Russian tanks ploughed through the countryside, leaving a mess of dirt and gravel behind.

The burning sensation in his legs increased with every move and he felt his muscles seize up. But he couldn't stop pedaling. First, they had to reach the ferry point and then they'd take it from there. So, he pushed through his agony, his exhaustion and the trembling of his legs, until the sweat ran in rivulets down his back.

With the sun high on the horizon, heat blazed down his back and he felt his tongue stuck against his palate. Just a little bit more...

"Richard, stop," Katrina said.

"I'm fine."

"At least drink some water," she answered with a soft voice.

He wanted to protest and say if he stopped now he might not be able to get his legs working again anytime soon. The road along the river was out in the open, with no shielding trees nearby. It was too exposed to stay and rest. They had to keep moving.

"Richard. Please stop," Katrina asked once more.

Richard groaned but stopped pedaling and brought the bicycle to a stop.

"Are you sick?" he asked when she gingerly climbed down.

"No, but you can't keep going this way." She put down the backpack and reached for the water bottle inside.

As soon as his feet hit the ground, he felt the earth swaying, much like a sailor did after weeks at sea. Dizziness took hold of him and he had to grab Katrina's shoulder to steady himself. Seeing the concern in her eyes, he said, "I'm fine. Just a bit tired."

The truth was he'd barely slept in two nights, and after pedaling for endless hours he could collapse and fall asleep before his body hit the ground.

"Let me pedal for a while," Katrina said.

"No, I'm fine." As much as he yearned for a break, he couldn't let her do the heavy lifting. With her petite stature, her feet would barely reach the pedals. Moving the two of them along on the old rusty thing was hard for a big man like him, let alone for someone half his size.

"You're not fine. Your face is white as a corpse, save for the red spots on your cheeks. You're about to pass out, if you don't stop. Trade me positions. Just for a little while. Please."

Seeing that she wasn't about to budge, he groaned and said, "Alright. You pedal."

She climbed on the saddle, her feet barely touching the pedals. But when he positioned himself on the crossbar, his big body overflowed the narrow space and she couldn't look around him. Neither could she properly move her legs.

"It doesn't work, so let me," he said, wondering how she'd ridden perched on the bar so many hours without complaining.

They stopped and switched positions again.

"Wait, I have an idea." She sat astride the crossbar and pushed her buttocks as far back as the space allowed. Then she put her feet on the pedals and said, "Now it works. Keep your legs out of reach and hold on tight."

He found a position to let his legs hang without scuffing the ground and put his arms around her waist for better balance. The monotonous ride and the blazing afternoon sun dulled his senses and he dozed off, tightening his grip around her waist as his body slumped against hers.

Several times he jerked awake when the bicycle rumbled through a pothole. But he simply couldn't force his eyes to stay open.

"Ouch!" He cried out as his bruised back hit the gravel with a painful thud. He looked around with bleary eyes and it took a few moments until he realized they'd both crashed to the ground, the bicycle coming to lie atop of them. "What happened?" He disentangled his sore limbs from the bicycle and then waited for Katrina to do the same, before he shoved it away and picked himself up off the hard ground.

"You fell asleep and tipped sideways, and I couldn't keep us upright." Katrina looked concerned. "Are you hurt?"

"I guess not…" He tried a crooked grin. "It doesn't feel much different now than before the fall. What about you?"

As always, she saw right through his attempts to put on a brave face. "I'm fine. A scratch on my shin and probably a bruise forming on my hip. But it's not me I'm worried about."

"Really, I'm fine." It was a lie and he had to bite his tongue to not scream with pain.

"You're such a bad liar." She pressed a kiss on his lips, dusted herself off and hauled the bicycle upright, struggling with the heavy weight.

Richard simply stood there, watching her efforts. He knew he should walk over and help her, but he just didn't have an ounce of strength left. Finally he managed to say, "I'm sorry. You might be right; I'm not in my best condition."

She turned around and giggled at him. "Not your best condition? The only time I've seen you worse is when I found you with the partisans, delirious with fever."

Shame spread across his body. *He* was the reason she'd ventured on this grueling trek. The last thing she needed was having him knocked out. It was only early evening and they would have daylight for another five hours at least. But despite that, it didn't make sense to continue.

"We should find a place to sleep and ride the rest of the way to the ferry in the morning," he said.

"Good idea. See that patch of trees over there?" She pointed into the distance and he nodded. "You sit here and wait while I refill the water bottle and then we'll push the bicycle to the trees."

He nodded again, stretching out on the grass while she ventured toward the riverbank for water. After a while he heard the clip-clopping of horses' hooves in the distance and he jerked upright, scanning the road. He saw nothing. But after several moments he heard it again, fragments of voices, carried by the wind. Probably another caravan of German refugees seeking to cross the Oder. But he thought it prudent to keep hidden until they knew whether the travelers were friend or foe.

Just when he set out in search for Katrina, she returned from the riverbank and he called out to her, "Quick, there's people coming."

For a moment, she looked surprised, but then hurried toward him, question marks in her eyes.

"I heard scraps of voices and clip-clopping of horses' hooves. We don't know who they are." Opportunists abounded. More than once they had observed groups of people taking advantage of others. With only the two of them they didn't stand a chance against a bigger group of looters wanting to rob them of their meager possessions. The best option was to get out of trouble's way.

Richard took the bicycle and pushed the heavy thing across the rough meadow toward the group of trees in the distance. Within minutes drops of sweat ran down his face and he cursed beneath his breath, but increased his efforts when the noise became louder.

When he turned to look at the road, there was nobody in sight. But the strangers would soon be visible, once they passed the bend about a mile further upstream.

"They're probably looking for the ferry as well," Katrina said, walking beside him, carrying the heavy rucksack.

"Perhaps."

Approximately fifteen minutes later, they reached the trees, and Richard dropped the bicycle into the grass, then collapsed against one of the trunks. Just as Katrina settled beside him, they saw the first of the horse-drawn carriages come around the bend.

"Expellees," Katrina said.

"Still, let's hide until they're gone."

They settled in the shadow with their backs to the road and Katrina unpacked the rucksack, distributing a slice of bread and ham to each of them.

"Eat and then sleep," she said, biting into her ration.

"And you?"

"Once the caravan is out of sight I'll refill our water and look out for plants to supplement our food." She smiled at him and he put his arm around her shoulders and pressed her against him. "What would I do without you, sweet woman?"

Without her, he'd probably be six feet under by now. Tortured to death. A shudder racked his body and he pressed her harder against him, blowing a kiss on her hair. "Thank you for saving my life – again."

"You're welcome. Now sleep."

He dropped momentarily into an exhausted sleep, stretched out on the comparatively soft grass.

CHAPTER 16

Katrina gazed at Richard's sleeping face. The pained grimace relaxed into an angelic expression as he drifted into a deep, and hopefully healing, sleep. She knew that he was doing his best to hide his injuries from her, so as not to worry her.

But she *was* worried, very much so. She'd seen the awful wounds and bruises on his back and guessed that at least some of his ribs were broken. She gave herself time to relax and leaned against the trunk, alone with her thoughts, waiting for the refugees to pass by.

Had she made the right decision by going with him? Should she have stayed? Returned to her parents' farm? Her heart grew weary with nostalgia, but one glance at Richard's face told her that wherever he was, that's where she wanted to be.

When the crowd had finally passed and disappeared behind a bend downstream, she got up, grabbed the water bottle and her shawl, and went to fetch water. On her way back, she trudged carefully through the meadow, searching for plants she could use for food or medicine. Dandelions and stinging nettle grew in abundance, and she filled her shawl with the leaves but still looked for something she could use to ease Richard's pain.

Keeping her eyes peeled upon the ground, she finally found something useful. A bunch of small, bright red blossoms atop a single stem. A subspecies of the Carthusian Pink – Dianthus carthusianorum. It was a staple in many monastery gardens because of its powerful pain-relieving properties. She picked a few of the plants, making sure they looked clean. At home she would have made an unguent, but now, a simple poultice would have to do.

She returned to find Richard completely passed out, and carefully unbuttoned his shirt. The ghastly sight of black-blue bruises and encrusted wounds brought tears to her eyes and she woke him up to get to work.

Richard remained half-asleep but obeyed her commands and followed her directions. She took off his shirt and placed her shawl beneath him. Rubbing one of the plants lightly between her fingers to break the skin and set the ingredients free, she placed it on the shawl.

"Lie down again," she said and helped him ease his back onto the makeshift bandage. Then she proceeded to distribute more Carthusian Pink across his ribs and abdomen with Richard already fast asleep. She wrapped the shawl around him, securing it tightly to keep the poultice in place. Since it was still warm out she didn't bother to put on his shirt or jacket and left that for later at night when the chill from the river would creep up to the meadows.

Katrina decided to get some sleep herself as well after

planning to continue their journey with the first light of dawn. She huddled down at his side and soon fell into a light sleep, her ears pricking up to any sign of danger. But nothing happened, except for other groups of refugees trekking by.

At the crack of dawn, Richard woke her with mock indignation on his face. "Admit it! You used me as guinea pig for your herbal medicine again."

Katrina giggled, relieved that he was in the mood to joke again. "Did it help?"

"How should I know? What was the purpose of your magic?" he said, a huge grin spreading from ear to ear.

"To ease the pain."

"Well, then it helped." He kissed her. "Thank you. Do you have something to ease my hunger, too?"

"In fact, I do." She pointed at the wilting dandelion and stinging nettle leaves beside the backpack.

"Ugh. What about a freshly roasted rabbit?"

"Sorry, no such thing. But you can have a slice of bread."

They ate the ration she distributed for each of them and despite Richard's hungry gaze at the food hidden inside the bag, he didn't complain and ask for more, but ate the green leaves with utter fearlessness.

As soon as they finished their morning meal, he stood and pushed the bicycle back to the road and invited her with a grand gesture. "Hop on, milady, we have an appointment to keep."

The road became increasingly damaged and every now and then the tires of the bicycle lost pressure and they had to climb down and use the hand pump clipped to the frame to pump up the tube.

Katrina welcomed the respites from sitting on the hard and uncomfortable crossbar, but she never once complained. The faster they reached the border, the better and safer they would be.

The farms and villages along the winding road were in a desolate condition and appeared as if the inhabitants had left long ago. Several hours upstream, they came up behind a slow-moving group. Initially, Katrina thought of overtaking them, but as they crested a small rise, the road leading to a lone ferry moving across the river unfolded in front of her eyes.

The road was packed with people, animals, and vehicles all the way down to the bank. Climbing from the bicycle, they walked to the end of the queue, watching as passengers poured from the ferry on the opposite bank, before it made a return trip, loading more refugees on its deck and heading across the river once again.

"That'll take us a while," she said, as they progressed slowly down the crest. She estimated the ferry to be three to four miles away.

"A while is good. We'll spend this night and maybe the next," Richard said.

He was right, of course. The ferry was excruciatingly slow and could only take so many people with each trip. Even if it didn't stop at night, they were in for a long, long wait.

Katrina suddenly felt extremely vulnerable in such a large group and she whispered, "I hope my countrymen don't decide to round us up here."

Richard put his arm around her shoulders. "They're probably glad we're showing them our heels and leaving their country. Why would they want to keep us from leaving?"

"Let's hope so, by goodness!"

As night fell, and the ferry stopped operations, everyone settled along the road to get some sleep. Despite her protests, Richard chatted to a large family.

When he returned to her side, he said, "It seems everyone here is headed to Görlitz. It's the only place to cross the Neisse River, far and wide. But rumor has it, there are too many refugees already and they can't cope with the constant influx of more people. The border closes for days on end, and apparently the border patrol are sending people back who don't have relatives in the Russian-occupied zone."

"What will we do?" Katrina asked.

"For now, continue with our plan. The rumors might not be true. And since Berlin lies in the Russian zone, I do have relatives there and they should let us pass through."

"If the border is open…"

"It's too early to worry now. Whatever we do, we need to head west. If Görlitz is closed, we'll find another place to cross the border."

An uneasy feeling took hold of her stomach, but she didn't dare voice her concern aloud. She leaned against him with a sigh, wishing she had his positive outlook on the world and could turn off her incessant worrying by taking things one step at a time. In contrast to his approach she'd already strategized twelve steps ahead and panicked over all the problems that could – and surely would – arise.

For one, he was a wanted man. A deserter without papers to prove otherwise. Richard might believe in miracles, but she couldn't fathom how the Russians would let him get away. She'd seen the signs hanging in Wroclaw that warned anyone hiding a Wehrmacht deserter.

"You worry too much, my love," he whispered into her ear, his hands rubbing her neck and shoulders, massaging the knots of anxiety away.

"Are you sure we shouldn't keep going further to see if there is another bridge?" Katrina asked later when they lay together along the roadside and studied the sheet Richard had torn from the atlas.

"No. A few miles downstream the Oder turns north and we need to go west. And haven't you seen the crowds pouring in from the other direction? If there was a bridge they would have used it."

"You're probably right." She snuggled against him, following his finger on the map. "Once we are on the other riverbank, it's less than seventy miles. And according to this map, there is, or at least used to be, a main road. If the road's in good condition, we might make it to Görlitz in two days."

"Or we might be in a traffic jam with all these people going the same way, unable to pass them by."

"Let's worry about that when we have crossed the river," Richard said and folded the map into his chest pocket. Then he pressed her against his chest. "Let's get some sleep."

Despite her best intentions to stop worrying, she lay there in the dirt, looking up at the stars in the sky. Richard lay on his side presenting her his backside, while he held on tight to the bicycle. She listened to his even breathing and snuggled tighter against him to keep herself warm.

Several yards away a baby cried, someone cursed, a

couple of people whispered, another person got up to pee...
It was anything but quiet this night. Still, she managed to
fall into a light slumber, using the rucksack with all their
possessions as a pillow, the strap secured to her arm.

The cry of the baby turned into an incessant, ear-
piercing wail, louder than an air raid siren. After a while she
couldn't stand it anymore and walked over to the mother of
the baby, who was rocking the little bundle back and forth,
desperately trying to stop the screaming.

"Is the child sick?" Katrina asked.

"He's having a fever and something's paining him." The
young woman gave her a helpless look.

"Can I see him, please?" Katrina touched the baby's forehead, finding it was burning up. His little cheeks were dark
red, but at least his wailing decreased when she massaged
his legs. "An infection, maybe a cold accompanied by joint
pains. Unfortunately there's not much I can do, but we
need to break the fever. Do you have a piece of cloth and
water?"

The young woman nodded, pointing at a small girl
sleeping crouched on the ground, her head resting on a
pillow. Katrina carefully moved the girl and took the pillow
that was stuffed with the family's clothing. She grabbed a
kerchief and drenched it in cold water, wrapping it around
the baby's left leg.

"Change it every couple of hours until the fever breaks.
And," she retrieved the remaining leaves of Carthusian Pink
from her rucksack, showing the woman what to do while
she explained, "rub one leaf between your fingers like this.
And then let your son suck at your finger. The oil will alle-
viate the pain and let him sleep."

"Thank you so much." The young woman was near to tears. "How can I ever pay you back for your kindness?"

Katrina smiled and said. "Show kindness to someone in need when you have the opportunity." Then she returned to Richard's side and finally fell asleep herself.

Late the next afternoon it was finally their turn to board the ferry. Katrina quietly listened to the gossip running wild. It seemed that the end of the war had set in motion an emigration of entire nations.

Three men, Churchill, Stalin and Roosevelt, had decided upon the fate of millions by a scratch of a pen. Vast lands in Poland's East now belonged to Russia, the Polish natives expelled to settle in the newly acquired regions in the west that formerly belonged to Germany, expelling the Germans from their homelands.

Where would all these homeless people go? Her fellow passengers jockeyed for superiority, representing outrageous numbers of displaced persons on the move, ranging from five to twenty million. It was such a vast number; she couldn't even fathom the sheer mass of people. But having seen the mass persecution and the hordes of fugitives, there was no doubt half of Europe was on the move.

CHAPTER 17

After a seemingly endless journey, the ferry ride took less than half an hour. Richard and Katrina were spewed ashore, holding hands tightly for fear of getting separated and never finding each other again.

Richard pushed the bicycle along in the stream of bedraggled people, all of them focused on their common goal: crossing the border into the safety of Germany. Everyone had a horrific story to tell, and although few people voiced their atrocious experiences, Richard could tell by the haunted look in their eyes.

He squeezed Katrina's hand tighter and said, "We need to get away from this crowd."

The next morning they woke before dawn and set off, passing the other travelling groups one by one, until they reached the head of the trekkers and mounted the bicycle again. They made good progress along the comparatively good road, and while the pedaling strained his legs, his ribs seemed to hurt less and he could even breathe without difficulties. Every few hours they would trade positions and he relaxed his burning muscles while Katrina did the back-breaking work.

When it was his turn again, he kept his gaze peeled to the ground, steering the bicycle between potholes and the trash lying around.

"Look, there's a sign!" Katrina shouted with excitement, all but causing him to lose balance as he looked up to decipher the rickety sign. It said, "Görlitz 10 Kilometers".

"We're almost there!" Katrina cried out in jubilation, pushing one arm high into the air.

Hope spread through his body, sending a warm feeling into every limb. Soon, they'd leave all this behind and find a place to settle down. He wondered whether he'd find his parents and sisters well and alive in their old apartment in Berlin.

He couldn't wait to wrap each of his loved ones into his arms and share the events of the past years. It had been almost eighteen months since he'd last received a letter from his mother, back when he'd been deployed to the rear-echelon in Lodz. Before he'd asked his superior to be transferred to the front again... and before his life had taken a turn he still couldn't get his head around.

"Hey! Watch out!" Katrina shouted just in time.

He swerved and steered the bicycle around a huge rock in the middle of the road. His heart thumping hard, he reminded himself to stay focused and not let his mind wander off to happier times.

Minutes later they encountered a bedraggled group walking east. Richard didn't think much of it, but when more travellers moved toward them, he stopped and climbed from the saddle.

Katrina cast him a questioning glance but followed suit.

"I'm trying to find out what's happening." He shoved the bicycle into her hands and sidled up to a group of middle-aged women with a bunch of children. There he picked out the single old man who apparently was the head of the group.

"Excuse me, mein Herr, why are you going East?"

The man looked at him with tired eyes and said, "The border in Görlitz is closed. Bloody Ivan isn't letting anyone cross the Neisse River, east or west. They say there are too many refugees already in the Soviet Zone. I saw it with my own eyes. There are hundreds of thousands stranded at the riverbank, unable to continue their journey."

"And where are you going now?"

"Honestly, I don't know. Find a place to rest and then decide," the man said.

"Isn't there another place to cross the river further north?"

"Not that I know of. Rumor has it there's no way but to swim across from here to Guben." That wasn't good news, but it could have been worse. From the town of Guben it wasn't far to Berlin.

"Do you know anything about Berlin?" Richard asked, hoping to get valuable information.

"No good, young man. The entire city is locked down. No one is getting in or out. The Allies are still fighting over who gets the best parts of the capital."

Richard couldn't hide his disappointment and the man asked, "What's your business there?"

"My family is in Berlin – if they're still alive."

"And you? Running away from the *Russenschreck?*"

Richard didn't fully trust the stranger, since Wehrmacht deserters evading Soviet captivity and those who helped them awaited severe punishment, so he said, "No. I escaped from one of the Polish concentration camps," leaving it unclear whether he meant a Nazi camp in Poland or the new camps where the Poles tortured Germans.

"If I were you, young man, I'd make over to the American sector. They treat our soldiers a lot better than the Ivan does." The man obviously didn't believe Richard's ruse.

"I'm not a soldier…" Richard protested.

"You're how old? Twenty? Prima facie evidence is against you. Unless you're a homosexual, a Jew or a criminal. In that case I'd still prefer the Ami over the Ivan."

"Thank you for the advice," Richard said and slowed his pace. He turned on his heel and returned to where Katrina waited with the bicycle. He found her talking to a pair of young women, who quickly bid their goodbyes when he showed up.

"Who was that?" he asked.

Katrina grinned. "Just two women trying to buy the bicycle."

"The old man said the border is closed."

"I know." She gestured for him to follow her and led him to a place several hundred yards away from the road. "We need to decide what to do next."

Richard nodded, watching the never-ending stream of refugees pouring down to the riverbank, where it came to a stop. From their vantage point he could see a few soldiers guarding the bridge, while masses of people flocked to both sides of the river. So the old man had been right. No crossing allowed – neither east, nor west. Tens of thousands caught in limbo.

"Those women said the Russians are meticulously checking the papers of every male between fifteen and sixty, sending them into captivity if they can't prove that they've never been drafted."

"I heard the same. The old man suggested that we make a beeline for the American sector, since they treat our soldiers a lot better than the Russians do."

"But they would still take you prisoner," Katrina said, passing him the bottle of water.

"I know, but it would only be for a short while, maybe a few months..." Richard knew that after the last war, the belligerent nations had started sending captured soldiers home as soon as the peace treaty had been signed.

"You don't know that. There's talk about using prisoners of war to rebuild the infrastructure."

"I don't mind serving time or even working for the Allies a year or two, if it helps mending the damage we caused. Just look at the destroyed lands we've passed through. Cities in ruins, fields devastated, even the forest was scorched in places." He'd never wanted to be a soldier, but like every one of his classmates, except for sickly, asthmatic Klaus, he'd been drafted the day he turned sixteen.

Shipped off to the Eastern front, he'd miraculously survived two years of gruesome battles, when so many others hadn't. Being captured and almost hanged by the Polish partisans had been a blessing in disguise, because it had allowed him to lie low and wait out the war pretending to be a Polish farmer by Katrina's side.

He'd never condoned the atrocities committed mostly by SS troops, but he'd never actively worked against Hitler either. He definitely shared responsibility for the destruction all round and felt a need to make up for it.

"If they take you prisoner, what about me?" Katrina's feeble voice interrupted his thoughts.

"You? Nothing will happen to you. You're a woman." She had nothing to worry about. The Allies didn't take civilians prisoner.

"But where will I go?"

Now it dawned on him. Since his family didn't know her, didn't have the slightest idea she even existed, they most likely wouldn't take her in if she arrived on her own.

He scratched his beard. "I could write you a letter for my family. After you give it to them to read, they'll take you in until I'm released."

She cast him an indulgent smile that clearly said she doubted the plan would work. A Polish woman on her own, roaming Germany to find her boyfriend's family. A family who didn't even know she existed, her only proof a letter from him.

"Then I'd better not get captured," he said, putting an arm around her shoulders.

"I'll be sure to let the authorities know that you'd rather not be imprisoned." Her voice dripped with sarcasm.

"Don't worry so much. We'll come up with something." He passed the water bottle back to her. "Do we still have food?"

"We do. You can have a piece of dried meat." She distributed the rations and then said, "But if we're on the road much longer, we're going to run out of food."

He took out the worn map from his chest pocket and unfolded it. He drew a line with his finger from North to South, starting with Karlsbad in the Sudetenland to Pilsen and down to Budweis in the Protectorate of Bohemia and Moravia, and said, "Apparently the Americans are here. They call it the demarcation line. It separates the American sector from the Russian sector."

"That's a long way," Katrina said, bending over the sheet of paper to get a better view.

"Yes, we'd have to follow the Neisse River south until its source and cross into the Sudetenland."

"I believe it's now called Czechoslovakia."

"Whatever the name, it used to belong to Germany and we should be safer there than in Poland." Richard chewed on the dried meat; the small slice Katrina had assigned him barely stopped the vicious grumble in his stomach.

"But what will we do once we are in the American sector?" she asked, biting a piece from her own slice of meat.

"Berlin is off limits. We can't go there." Sorrow for his family flooded his heart. They might be stuck in what currently seemed to be the worst hellhole on earth.

"That's what the two women told me as well. Nobody knows for how long, though." She gazed at the last bite of her meat and then shoved it into his mouth.

"Thank you, sweetheart." He knew he should have protested her sacrifice, but he was too hungry to even pretend. They sat a few minutes in silence, each one of them hanging onto their own thoughts.

"From Karlsbad it isn't too far into Munich and we

could go to my Aunt Lydia's farm in Lower Bavaria. There we'll be safe."

"But won't she mind the two of us imposing on her?" she asked.

He laughed. "You don't know her. She and her husband have a big farm and she'll probably be delighted at having more helping hands for harvesting season."

Katrina made a pensive face and then said, "My grandparents used to hire lots of seasonal hands for harvest. But that was before my parents sold off most of the land and kept only the fields around the house."

"Well, Lydia's farm has several acres of fields and cows and pigs…" He was transported back to happy childhood days when he and his younger sister Lotte had spent the summers with Aunt Lydia and her ever-growing flock of children. He and Lotte had chased each other up the trees, played hide-and-seek in the forest, frolicked for hours in the nearby lake, and done everything children liked to do that adults weren't supposed to know about.

"You're smiling," Katrina said.

"Yes, I had fun times with Aunt Lydia, Uncle Peter and their many children."

"Peter?" Katrina's eyes filled with sadness. He knew that she still hoped her own brother Piotr was alive. He'd been an officer in the Polish Army and disappeared weeks after Hitler's invasion in 1939.

Richard reached for her hand and said, "I hope you'll see him again."

She dabbed at her eyes, taking a few moments to compose herself. "So we'll try our luck reaching Karlsbad?"

"Yep."

"How far is it?" She glanced at him.

On the map it looked small, about half the span of his hand. He calculated the distance in his head and said, "About one hundred fifty miles, give or take. Let's ride a few more hours south and find a place to sleep away from all the people," he suggested.

"That's a good plan. We need to go to the river anyways and fill our bottle with water."

He grinned. "Always better to do this upstream of a mass of defecating people."

"Richard!" She playfully slapped him on his arm and he kissed her, taking the opportunity to whisper a sweet threat into her ear, "I can't wait until we're alone tonight and I'll show you what happens to a bad girl who slaps her man."

"We're not married yet, mister! And I can slap you all I want for behaving badly." She tried to keep a serious face but he could see the laughter in her eyes.

"Well, you haven't seen me behave badly yet. But you will as soon as we're under the cover of darkness." He nibbled on her earlobe and pressed her chest against his to emphasize his words. The goosebumps breaking out on the skin of her neck made him yearn for the sun go down.

CHAPTER 18

R iding the bicycle fast became Katrina's second nature. Even sitting perched on the hard crossbar didn't hurt that much anymore. When the sun shone down on them and there was nobody else in sight, she sometimes started to sing a song.

Once in a while Richard would join her, but usually he'd just hum or whistle the melody. She taught him some of her favorite Polish nursery songs to keep them both entertained on their long days of travel. For their safety, they always kept away from big accumulations of people.

They'd soon found out that the situation in the new Czechoslovakia was even worse than in Poland. The Czechs, who'd been viciously oppressed throughout the war, had gone on a killing frenzy that surpassed what she'd seen in Wroclaw in terms of cruelty, brutality and methodology. All Germans were forced to wear white armbands, making them an easily identifiable target whenever the new masters were baying for blood.

So they kept to themselves, always seeking out the smaller roads, never venturing inside bigger towns, even though this slowed down their progress toward the demarcation line.

Four days after changing their plans they'd used up the last morsel of their food and solely depended on what they could gather along the way, which wasn't much. Hunger was a constant companion and oftentimes they couldn't find clean water to drink. But the goal of reaching safety in the American sector propelled them forward, day after day. Pedaling all day, sleeping huddled together at night.

"What do you think, how long until we reach Karlsbad?" she asked.

"Hmm, another three or four days maybe?" he said, skidding to a stop at a fork in the road. One road led to the right, climbing toward the mountains towering above them, the other one to the left, down into the flatlands.

"Which road to take?" he asked.

"The one to the left looks better, but it's not exactly our direction." She spotted a tiny village a few hundred yards down. "What if I go and ask?"

"I'll go with you," he said.

"No, I'm safer on my own." She knew he hated letting her go on her own, but she'd have better chances of finding a friendly person without him. Since Polish and Czech were similar languages she could understand about two thirds of what the locals said, if they spoke slowly and clearly. And nobody would mistake her for one of the abhorred Germans. She walked down to the village and saw a group of women scrubbing laundry.

"Excuse me? I got lost. Can you tell me which way to get

to Karlsbad?"

"You're not from around here," one of the women said, eying her suspiciously.

"I'm from Poland, the Nazis abducted my family and I'm searching for them. Their last known location was Karlsbad."

"The name's Karlovy Vary," an older woman with a sharp nose said.

"I'm sorry, of course that's the correct name, now that we defeated the Nazi swine," Katrina said in an attempt to appease the woman.

"You defeated them? Who are you? Joan of Arc?" The woman laughed out loud, apparently seeking a quarrel.

"Not me personally, although I used to have a farm back in Poland, feeding our brave partisans."

"So why haven't you stayed on your farm?" a young woman said.

Katrina swallowed down a snide remark and forced a pleasant smile on her face, giving thanks to the fact she'd insisted Richard not come with her. These village women would have eaten him alive. "SS thugs torched my farm and abducted my family. I'm searching for them."

"Go home, girl. This is no place for a woman on her own. Too many German refugees who can't be trusted."

Katrina's smile froze on her lips. *It's not the German refugees I'm afraid of.*

"Let her go, if she wants. It's her life," another woman chimed in, and added, "The shortest way is going up from where you came and turn left. That small road reaches Karlovy Vary via the Ore Mountains. But it's a treacherous and steep path that's only passable during the summer months." She seemed to sense Katrina's hesitation and said, "Or you could follow this road down to the lowlands. Once you're in Prague you take a turn west to Karlovy Vary. It's the longer route, but probably still faster and a lot safer."

Katrina doubted it was safer for Richard and her in the capital than in the back country, but she politely thanked the women and returned to the place where Richard waited for her.

"Damn," Richard cursed, after she relayed her information to him, "all fucking roads lead to Prague."

"And I thought that was Rome," she said, trying to lighten the mood.

He cast her a dark stare. "We don't want to go into Prague. You said it yourself. Even these villagers are out for German blood. This whole bloody country is completely out of control."

While she had to agree with him, she couldn't help but say, "It's kinda your own fault. If your country hadn't assaulted all of Europe, none of this would have happened."

Richard's brooding stare became even darker and he mumbled something she couldn't understand. She let him work out his anger and patiently waited until the mumbling stopped and he scratched his beard. "We'll take the mountain route."

Katrina shook her head. "Are you sure? It will be tedious; we might not be able to use the bicycle."

He kept scratching his beard, until he finally looked up at her. "We'll try. Pray that we don't get lost."

A shudder caught her shoulders. Could they really get lost in the mountains? Surely there were roads to follow. "Do you think there are wolves?"

His face broke into a teasing smile. "I guess so. Wolves, and bears maybe."

"You're kidding, right?" She involuntarily took a step backwards, wrapping her arms around herself.

"I've never been in the Erzgebirge, but I wouldn't be surprised if there were. Although they usually don't attack humans."

"Usually?" Anxiety sucked the breath out of her lungs and the idea of taking the mountain route became even less appealing.

Richard cast her a reassuring smile. "I prefer a wolf over a horde of bloodthirsty Czech partisans any time of the day."

Uncertain of the viability of their new plan, she reluctantly climbed on the bicycle. They followed the small trail up into the mountains. Soon it became too steep to pedal and they had to push the bicycle. Sweat dripping down her forehead and her arms, she wished for a cooling swim in a lake. Not that they'd seen any lakes in days. After several hours of climbing, they found the road swallowed by a mud avalanche. As far as she could see, there was only debris.

Richard yelled several German curse words she didn't understand, the echo from the mountains sending shudders down her spine. He then flopped to the ground, hiding his face in his hands.

She sidled up to him, putting a hand on his shoulder. "I'm sorry."

"It's not your fault, but we won't find our way through without a local guide."

"So we'll just sit down and wait until one comes along?"

"Ha, very funny."

Richard looked so miserable, it squeezed her heart. "We'll have to take the road to Prague then."

"I guess we must." He still made no effort to get up and she worried he'd have a breakdown.

She'd been close to a breakdown herself many times during this journey and every time it had been Richard's calm strength that had brought her back to sanity. But apparently even his positivity had limits. It was time for her to take the lead.

"It might not be that bad. We can both pretend to be Polish slave workers on our way home." He raised his head, a sliver of hope entering his eyes as he listened to her plan. "The Czechs won't notice your accent, and we can still understand each other because the languages are so similar."

"It might work. Two slave workers on their way home. It's just that we're traveling in the wrong direction." He squinted his eyes and she knew he was trying to figure out a solution.

"We can always say we got lost or the road was blocked and we had to retreat and go around," she suggested.

"Blocked by a mud avalanche you mean?" Finally, he was smiling again.

"That's the spirit!" Katrina gave a silent sigh, relieved to see his determination return. She had no idea what she'd have done if he had an actual breakdown.

They mounted the bicycle and rushed down the slope, the air stream blowing into their faces. She felt her cheeks heat up with the thrill of the downhill race and forgot about her sorrows – at least for a little while.

~

The next morning, they continued their journey toward Prague with the intention of giving the capital as wide a berth as possible. Katrina could already see the city in the distance when they stopped at yet another crossing that gave them the option of going straight into Prague or right to Pilsen.

Pilsen wasn't their intended destination, but what difference did it make where they crossed the demarcation line into the American sector? Pilsen was as good as Karlsbad in her eyes and if the distance to cover was less, all the better.

"Let's head for Pilsen," she said, excitement in her voice, when she noticed another sign a few meters further away that struck terror into her heart and mind.

"Richard, do you see that sign?"

He turned his head and nodded gravely. The sign read:

Warning – To the German Soldier:

Report immediately to the Military Government. If you are caught attempting to escape identification by wearing civilian clothes you may be shot as a spy.

To the German Civilian:

If you have helped stragglers from the German army, in accordance with instructions from the Allies, report them immediately to the Military Government. Any failure on your part to do so is a crime under the laws of Military Government and may be punished by the heaviest penalty.

"We knew that already, although this part here is reassuring," Richard said, reading out loud the small print at the bottom of the sign, "German soldiers are treated as Prisoners of War in accordance with the Geneva Convention. They will be sent home as soon as possible after the end of the war."

"Maybe those who're captured by the Amis, but the Russians will use them to rebuild their infrastructure. We've seen endless transports going east," Katrina said.

"That much is true. I'd rather turn myself in to the Amis... if we ever reach that damn demarcation line." Richard wasn't the only one who thought so. They'd met countless stragglers trying to do exactly that. No man – or woman – wanted to end up in Russian captivity. Even though nothing certain was known, the much-touted *Russenschreck* bedeviled the Wehrmacht soldiers.

He pulled out the map and unfolded it. "Assuming we're right here, it shouldn't be more than seventy miles."

"That's more than we can cover in a day," Katrina murmured needlessly and mounted the bicycle, as Richard changed their direction and started pedaling once more. But throughout the rest of the day the stark words on the warning sign plagued her. Richard was walking on thin ice and both of them could be found out and punished.

"We'll be fine. You have to have faith," he said.

Faith in what? Her faith had been tested too many times during the war years, but she didn't utter her doubts and instead said, "I'll be forever grateful to Edmund and Barbara for giving me the bicycle. Who knows where we'd be now without it."

"Your relatives most certainly did us a huge favor," Richard agreed.

Katrina nodded. "Would you like me to pedal for a while?"

"Not right now. Just relax and enjoy the ride while you can."

CHAPTER 19

Richard kept a steady pace, his legs doing the now familiar work like an automaton. Most of his bruises and wounds had healed, but he didn't have any illusions about what would be inflicted upon him should he ever have to experience the hospitality of the Czechs.

The ruse of being former slave workers was flimsy at best, and he decided it was best not to test its credibility.

"There's a checkpoint up ahead," Katrina warned him and he brought the bicycle to a screeching halt. To both sides of the road lay flat lands as far as the eye reached. There was no way they could sidestep the checkpoint.

"We'll have to take our chances," he said sullenly.

"This was bound to happen," Katrina replied. "We stick to our story of being Polish slave workers on our way home. The Soviets won't pick up your accent."

Fatalism spread across Richard's body and he said, "Alright then."

He pedaled the several hundred yards up to the road-block and then came to a halt in front of two heavily armed Soviet soldiers.

"Stop! Papers," one of the soldiers demanded, while the other one pointed his rifle at them.

It had been a while since Richard had last stared into the muzzle of a Mosin Nagant, and back then he'd held his own weapon in hand. It was an entirely different feeling now. And he didn't like it one bit.

He held the bicycle while Katrina carefully slid down, talking in Russian to the soldier and producing her paperwork from their bag. The man perused her identification with a quick glance and then asked, "You're Polish?"

"Yes."

Richard climbed from the saddle and leaned the bicycle against the roadblock before he approached the soldier.

"Papers!" the soldier demanded, nodding at Richard.

Richard used the few Russian words he knew, "No papers. Stolen."

The soldier's brows shot up and his eyes took on a suspicious glint. "No papers?"

"No, ser…" Richard caught himself in the last moment before he pronounced the military rank and instead said, switching to Polish, "…sir. I was robbed near Prague and my papers stolen."

The sergeant became frustrated with the mutual lack of language skills and gazed at Katrina. "You! Translate!"

She dutifully did so, but the Russian didn't buy into the story. "Your friend was robbed, they stole his papers but left the bike?"

"No, the bicycle belongs to her," Richard said, glad for the delay in communication caused by Katrina having to translate everything. It gave him time to think about a believable cover story.

"You were robbed, but she wasn't? How's that possible?" the soldier asked in disbelief.

"We got separated when crossing the Moldavia in Prague and only caught up to each other the next day. Thankfully she had the bicycle and one of our bags, because the thieves left me with nothing but the clothes I'm wearing."

"Where are the two of you headed?"

"Home to Poland," Katrina lied so effortlessly; Richard had to admire her guts.

The muzzle of the Mosin-Nagant pointed slightly downwards, but the second soldier still had his full attention on them.

"And where do you come from?" their interrogator asked.

Again, it was Katrina who gave the answer. "We were abducted by the Nazis and had to work for them in a factory near Munich."

Richard had difficulties keeping a straight face. Where on earth had she learned to lie with such grace?

"Damn Nazi swine," the Russian said, spitting at the ground.

Even without Katrina's translation Richard understood and nodded. "Yes. Nazi swine."

A short glance of understanding crossed between the men and Richard physically felt the tension easing off. Moments later, the soldier lifted the rifle.

Katrina gave the two soldiers a sheepish look. "We just want to get home to our families."

"I get it. Everyone wants the same thing. Find out about their loved ones." The sergeant had a nostalgic look in his eyes, as he was probably thinking about his own family.

"Now, you do know you are turned around?" the other soldier said.

"What?" Richard feigned innocence. He made a show of turning around, looking at the mountains in the distance and then turning back to the soldier with a puzzled look on his face. "We're going the wrong direction?"

"Yes. Poland is that way." The soldier pointed off to where they had come from.

"I told you we took a wrong turn," Katrina said and bestowed a smile upon the Russians. "Everything was so chaotic and we fled, grateful to get out of the melee with our lives."

The soldier still watched Richard carefully. Finally, he beckoned them to come with him to the top of the little hill the road was on. He pointed up to the right saying, "You could return to Prague or take the shortcut up here. There's a fork in the road further down. Take the left and it'll lead you round that hill and back east."

"Thank you so much," Katrina said after the Russian told them they were free to go.

They hurried back to where they'd left the bicycle at the checkpoint, just to see it being wheeled away by two Czech partisans. The thugs had the audacity to wave at them before they mounted the vehicle.

Richard yearned to go after them, but one glance at the grinning faces of the Russian soldiers told him that causing any sort of ruckus wouldn't be a good idea. Gritting his teeth, he grabbed Katrina's hand and pulled her down the road in the direction of Pilsen.

Seventy more miles on a bicycle hadn't seemed so bad, but walking the entire distance was a whole different story. Anger and disappointment took hold of every cell in his body, making breathing difficult and clouding his mind. He fumed under his seemingly calm exterior, but as always Katrina picked up on his mood and said, "It doesn't help to get angry now. There's nothing we can do."

"They stole it right under our noses, with the Ivan watching... and laughing." He wished he could turn around, find the thieves and give them a good beating. But alas, that wasn't going to happen.

"It served us well for the biggest part of the journey. I'm sure we can walk the rest on foot. We've walked farther than that in Poland." Katrina grimaced.

"Yes, but..." There were a million buts, but one glance at her resolute expression made him shut down. It was best not to waste his breath on things he couldn't change.

"We're still alive and they believed our ruse," Katrina said, gazing at him. "And it does make for a nice change, not having to perch on the crossbar."

He chuckled, overwhelmed by her resolve to see the silver lining and took her hand. "Care to take a walk with me, beautiful lady?"

"Why, I'd love to," she giggled, the silliness a way to relieve the tension the meeting with the Russian soldiers had caused in both of them.

He pressed a kiss on her lips. "I love you, Katrina

Zdanek. Thank you for putting up with me. With you by my side I'll go up against everything and anyone."

"I love you, too."

CHAPTER 20

O ver the course of the next few days they walked and
walked.

And walked.

Sometimes they would come across some Wehrmacht
stragglers, headed in the same direction, but they never
joined one of those groups for longer than a few minutes of
exchanging information.

At night, they slept cuddled next to one another, exhaustion and fear swallowing the need for words. Despite the
oppressive heat in the early summer nights, Katrina snuggled as tight against Richard as possible, listening to his
heartbeat and falling asleep with the confidence that he
loved her no matter what.

She never once regretted her decision to leave Poland
behind, because she couldn't fathom a life without the man
she loved by her side.

With him, she was sure, she'd feel at home anywhere.
The only thing she wished for was a roof above her head

and freedom. And no longer being oppressed by the Nazis or persecuted by those who hated them. She rubbed her hand across her abdomen with a smile. As soon as they reached his aunt's farm she'd tell him about the sweet secret she carried beneath her heart.

In the morning she was awakened by a chirping sound and opened her eyes to find a couple of birds sitting on a tree nearby. Sunlight filtered through the trees and the air smelled of summer, innocence and hope.

She leaned over to wake Richard with a kiss but found his eyes already open. He caught her around the waist and rolled them over, coming to lie atop of her.

"Hey, you're getting me all dirty," she protested.

"As if you could get any dirtier than you already are." He chuckled and proceeded to trail kisses down her neck.

As much as she liked his caresses, she pushed him away. "You seem to have forgotten that we are in flight. We need to get on the road."

He pouted and rolled off of her, but made no attempt to get up.

"Come on. Contrary to popular belief this is not a summer vacation," she said.

"It could be. If only my companion would impose a slightly less stringent regime."

She sighed in mock exasperation. "At least one of us has to stay strong. We can make all the love you want once we're safe on the other side of the border."

"Now, that is a promise I won't forget." He laughed and made to get up, but not before pressing another heated kiss on her lips.

Katrina shook her head at his antics, but she did so with

a smile. Then she ventured deeper into the forest to take care of business. On her way back she heard a gurgling sound and followed its direction. Several dozen yards away she came across a creek with brilliant clear water and bent down to drink her fill before she called out, "Richard, come here!"

Without waiting for him, she stepped out of her skirt and blouse to wash up after so many days of walking covered in sweat and grime. She was standing only in her undergarments when he showed up.

"A forest nymph. What a nice surprise. Does that mean you have changed your mind about having sex?" A broad grin spread across his face.

She splashed him with some of the cool water. "No, you wicked man. Now come here, and wash off your dirt."

"My body may be cleansed, but my mind will always entertain dirty thoughts when you're around." He grinned some more, grabbed her with both arms and pressed her against his chest.

Giggling, she struggled to free herself and they both fell into the calf-deep water. It was chilly, but a wonderful refreshment after another night that didn't seem to cool down.

"Now see what you've done," she said as she looked down on her soaked undergarments.

"And here I thought you wanted to wash up." He put an arm beneath her head and captured her mouth in a passionate kiss, while his free hand ventured beneath her camisole.

She was lying in the cool creek, gurgling water rushing past her body and Richard's expert hands awakening the flames of passion in her. *What the heck*, she thought. Who cared whether they hit the road half an hour later? She softened her resolve and let her body melt against his.

He didn't need more of an invitation to divest her of her remaining undergarments and make sweet love to her.

Later, she scrubbed their clothes in the clear water, and then Richard wrung them out. The morning air hung warm between the trees, and the sun in the cloudless sky above them promised another scorching day.

"Isn't it an amazing feeling to be clean again?" she said, stepping into her wet clothes.

"It definitely is. I'd already forgotten how light my skin is when it's not caked in grime." Richard grimaced as he stepped into his squeaking trousers. "Although I could do without the wet pants."

"They'll dry soon enough. Now let's get going. We have a few dozen more miles to go." Katrina filled the water bottle one last time and handed him the rucksack.

"You don't think there's something to eat in there?" he asked with a hopeful glance.

"I'm afraid not. I've turned it inside out several times by now and haven't found anything remotely edible."

His disappointed expression stabbed her heart. How she wished she could conjure up a loaf of bread or a rabbit to roast.

In the afternoon they came upon on a slower-moving bunch of German refugees. In contrast to the scattered groups of young males, this group definitely consisted of civilians. Ancient men, women of all ages and children. They were pushing and shoving their belongings on bicycles, wheelbarrows, and prams. Anything with wheels.

"Don't you think we should join this group?" Katrina asked, still reeling from their encounter with the Russian soldiers several days ago.

"We'd only make ourselves a target. With just the two of us we have a better chance of going undiscovered by the Czechs," he said.

"I know. But we should arrive in Pilsen by tomorrow and in a big group like this, you wouldn't stick out so much. We'd have a much better chance of getting across the border with a big group of refugees than on our own."

He bit on his lip and she could read his thoughts. "We can still find a group to join near the border."

"What if there isn't one? Lingering about the border will only draw attention to us." Truth be told, she hated the thought of joining one of the groups, because if caught by partisans with a group, they couldn't pretend to be Poles. That would only make things worse. But on the other hand, if the Americans suspected Richard was a Wehrmacht straggler, they'd send him back to the Russians. And God only knew what would happen to her.

His face clearly showed the various emotions fighting for dominance, until he said, "Alright, we'll join them, but at the first sign of trouble we break away."

Katrina sighed. When would this nightmare end? Would she ever be able to walk down a street without looking back over her shoulder?

They walked another day with the group of refugees, getting friendly with them, pretending to be Germans who'd been forced to flee their hometown Breslau, now called Wroclaw. The people on the trek were Sudeten, folks that had lived in this area many centuries, cultivating their

German heritage, but had been tossed from one nation to another by the whims of fate since the beginning of this century.

After the last World War the government of the new multi-ethnic state of Czechoslovakia had done its best to make the Germans feel unwelcome and even persecuted in the new country. This, in turn, had led to the annexation of the Sudetenland into the German Reich in 1938, condoned by England and France in the Munich Agreement. The Germans had gained the upper hand and treated the Czechs with the same cruelty and disdain they'd experienced from the Czechs throughout the two decades before.

Katrina shook her head. When would people learn to coexist in peace instead of hate and fear of everyone who spoke a different language, followed a different God or religion, or looked different?

Now that Germany was a dying country, experiencing the last twitches before its inevitable demise, these refugees who had been expelled from their homes feared that they'd never return. Neither dead nor alive. Once more the old quarrel between Germans and Czechs flared up, with even more cruelty than ever before.

She ducked her head between her shoulders, her gaze piercing the earth in front of her feet. She didn't belong. Not with the refugees, not with those who expelled them. She was a foreign object, swept to this location by the tides of war – and love.

Her only reason to be here stood beside her. Her hand searched for his, wanting to feel the safety of his physical presence, to feel that he wouldn't leave her alone.

"An American flag!" someone yelled, and the exhausted

group stopped for a moment to look. Nobody cheered, probably because they didn't have any energy left.

According to Richard's calculations they were still more than a dozen miles away from Pilsen, but some of the older youths, who had been sent ahead as scouts, soon returned and explained the situation.

"The actual demarcation line is in the small town of Rokycany, while the first town entirely in the American sector is Pilsen," a girl of about fourteen years explained. "It's just across the river, but the bridge is only open during the day from eight to six."

"We'll find a place to settle for the night and line up for the crossing first thing in the morning," the leader of the group decided after eyeing the position of the sun in the sky.

Richard squeezed Katrina's hand and whispered into her ear, "We have arrived."

"Yes, my dear," she said, not wanting to put a damper on his good mood. Although they could see the American lines, they were far from having arrived. The Soviets and the Americans had made an agreement stipulating that all German soldiers found west of the American stop line by one minute after midnight on May 9 would become American prisoners and those found east of that line would be Soviet prisoners.

The part of the agreement that concerned her most was that any German soldier caught infiltrating American lines after that deadline would be turned over to the Soviets. They'd heard of men who'd gotten as far into the Reich as Regensburg, one hundred miles behind the stop line, and had been returned to the Russian sector.

Along the main roads several roadblocks had been set up to stem the tide of surrendering Wehrmacht soldiers and prevent them from sneaking through American lines. Richard only stood a chance if they could make the border patrol believe that he was indeed a civilian.

It didn't take long until the trek stopped again and the leader decided to camp at the bank of a tiny lake just outside Rokycany. This was just fine with Katrina, as she was tired to the bone, her stomach a huge gnawing hole. At least she could fill it with water and then fall into a death-like sleep.

"Come here," Richard whispered and patted the place on the ground next to him. She dropped down and was fast asleep even as he wrapped his arm around her.

CHAPTER 21

Richard was awakened by sneaking steps and jerked up, his eyes piercing the darkness of the night. Nothing to see, nor hear. But his neck hair stood on end with the certainty that someone, or something, was observing him.

He fumbled for his knife, but even before he'd reached it in the darkness, he felt a cold blade against his throat as a whispered voice threatened, "Don't even think about it. The less you resist, the better for you."

Richard pressed out a throaty agreement and slowly raised his hands. Moments later several dozen dark figures approached the sleeping group of travelers and with the cordon tightened around the camp, the thieves proceeded to relieve the refugees of anything of value they owned.

A woman screamed, but the scream stopped suddenly and from then on, nobody dared to make a single sound, leaving the camp in an eerie silence only interrupted by short commands to hand over the valuables.

Out of the corner of his eye, he saw how Katrina handed over their only possession, the rucksack with the water bottle and some extra clothing. The robber turned it inside out and, angry at the lack of anything of material value, hit Katrina in the face.

She fell backwards and hit her head, screaming with pain, "*Psiakrew!*"

All the blood drained from Richard's face as he realized how the thug turned toward her with a shining knife in his hand. He didn't quite understand the man's words, but the way she crept backwards indicated an explicit threat.

Katrina lay on the ground, her head throbbing with pain, but that was nothing compared to the fear that grabbed her heart as she realized the mistake she'd committed.

"You must see this, Karol," the man who'd hit her called out. Moments later a huge man with black hair and a pistol in his left hand approached them with face grim.

"What's so important?" Karol said impatiently.

"This one. She's not a bloody German."

"Not a German. Well…" Karol smirked. He leaned forward, his foul breath skimming her face.

Katrina tried to creep away from him, but bumped into the boots of another man. She was effectively trapped in place. Richard sat several feet away from her, a knife to his throat, watching her with panic-stricken eyes.

"What's your name?" Karol asked, setting his pistol on her chest when she didn't immediately answer.

"Katharina Klausen," she lied.

"Lying bitch." A boot connected with her ribs and she gave a short yelp, but swallowed down another Polish expletive that had brought her into this terrible position in the first place. "Where are you from?"

"Breslau," she managed to press through gritted teeth.

"A Polish Nazi whore," Karol said, kicking her again.

"I'm not..." Katrina stopped herself, the futility of the situation washing over her in waves. She'd lose either way. Whether they killed her for being one of the despised Germans or because they thought her to be a Nazi collaborator didn't really matter in the end.

"Was getting shagged by that piece of trash worth dying for?" Karol pointed at Richard with a dirty leer.

"Please, this is a mistake, let me go," she pleaded with him.

"Maybe I could do that," he said, skimming his pistol down her abdomen until he pushed it between her legs. "But first you have to tell me who you really are." The hard muzzle pressed up against her soft flesh.

She squirmed, but willed her body to become limp as the pressure of the revolver against her core increased. She had no idea what to tell him. He'd shoot her either way.

"Ahh, why suddenly so silent, you Nazi whore? Afraid of your death already? Do not fear, you'll live long enough to run the gauntlet in town." He removed his pistol, brutally kicking his boot into her sides, before he ordered, "Hogtie her and take her down to the market place with the other collaborators."

The next moment, two hands grabbed her and threw her over a man's shoulder, and he carried her away like a sack of flour, before he threw her atop the pile of booty on a lorry. With a shiver, she looked back on the image that would haunt her for the rest of her days. Richard's pale face and blood splattering from his throat. Leaden bleakness settled in her soul and she closed her eyes, praying for a quick end.

CHAPTER 22

A sharp pain sliced at Richard and then the man holding him disappeared. Instinctively he raised his hand to his throat, feeling warm liquid running down his fingers. Barely able to see through his rage, he heard the Czechs leaving with their booty – and Katrina.

He shot up to go after them, but dizziness swayed him and he found himself back on the earth, one person holding him and a female voice saying, "Quick, give me something to dress the wound."

A tearing sound and moments later the woman wrapped a piece of cloth around his neck. He stirred again, but she held him down and said, "You have to lie still. It's only a surface cut, but it has to stop bleeding before you can get up."

So he wouldn't die just yet. Which meant he had to live with the torment of what he'd just allowed to happen.

"Katrina..." he whispered.

"Best to forget about her," the woman said with averted eyes.

Forget? How could he forget about the love of his life?

"We'll leave after dawn and line up to cross the demarcation line. You're welcome to come with us." She cast him a sheepish smile. "You don't have proper papers, am I right?"

Richard nodded resigned.

"Don't worry, we'll say you're one of us. You'll reach safety in no time at all."

He didn't say anything so as not to annoy the kind woman, but he wouldn't sit idly by and escape to Germany while Katrina was murdered in town.

Someone put a cup of water into his hands and he greedily drank it, glad when the swallowing movement didn't seem to tear open his fresh wound. At least the pulsating throb had stopped, and he assumed the cut had closed and wasn't bleeding anymore. He could call himself lucky that the bandit hadn't cut deeper into his throat.

At the command of the leader of the refugee trek, everyone packed their belongings for the imminent departure, wiped snotty noses, ordered children to stay in line and tethered babies to the haphazard vehicles.

Richard went to search for their rucksack and found it lying empty in the dirt. All their other possessions had been trampled to pieces and dispersed across the campgrounds. He couldn't even find the water bottle, but he found a tiny pocketknife. It wasn't much longer than his thumb and not an adequate replacement for the dagger he'd possessed, but it would surely come in handy one day. Then he slunk away from the group of Germans and followed the road the partisans had taken into Rokycany.

Dawn broke over the land and he could see the American flags wafting in the distance. Fear attacked him, holding him in its leaden grip, and for a moment his resolve to find Katrina softened. It would be so easy to return to the trekkers and cross the border with them. He'd be safe in their midst, free to search for his family. But at what cost? He'd never be able to look into the mirror again if he didn't try and find Katrina. Hadn't she been prepared to offer herself as payment for his freedom just weeks ago?

The moment of weakness passed and he hastened his steps, afraid he wouldn't find the place where they publicly punished the collaborators.

He shouldn't have worried, as even this early in the morning, a huge mass of cheering, shouting and brawling locals gathered at what seemed to be the main town square, next to the line where Americans and Russians each marked their conquered territories in Europe. He had the feeling that neither army would leave their newly acquired lands anytime soon.

Then he saw her and the cut in his throat began throbbing with the pulse of his rage. Katrina sat tethered to a chair, alongside two other women, forced to watch the Czech tormenters shear the first woman's hair, rather viciously, with a butcher's knife. The cheering crowd swallowed her screams.

When the knife-wielding pig turned toward Katrina, Richard balled his hands into fists. As her beautiful brunette hair fell down her sides, blood started streaming from the cuts on her bald head. Even from this distance he could see how she held back her tears and cries of pain, too proud to give the bastards the satisfaction of knowing they'd broken a defenseless woman.

Helplessly, he stood rooted to the ground and watched. When all the women had been shorn, they were unshackled from their chairs and led through the crowd, with their hands tied behind their backs. The crowd spat at the miserable souls and started chanting, "Hang they must! Hang they must!"

All the blood drained from Richard's head and he must have looked paler than skim milk as he put his feet into motion, shoving through the crowd to reach Katrina.

"Hey! I was here first," someone yelled, but Richard didn't care and continued to elbow his way through to the woman he loved. Just when he'd reached her, a group of Russian soldiers stepped onto the podium and he breathed a sigh of relief.

But the soldiers didn't think about restoring order and instead settled onto the chairs, enjoying a vantage point for the gallows on the other side of the square. Someone shoved at Richard, who lost his footing and stumbled against the man leading Katrina to the gallows.

"Get out of my way, brute!" the man hissed and stepped aside.

Seizing the moment, Richard lunged at Katrina and took her down with his fall, pressing the tiny pocketknife into her hands. He never managed to see her face, but he had to hide a proud smile when the knife disappeared in her palm within the blink of an eye.

"Sorry," Richard said to her guard and faded back into the crowd as she was manhandled up and toward the gallows. Now... he watched... waited.

And prayed.

~

Katrina grasped the knife, relishing the feel of the cold metal. She hadn't been able to see the person who'd shoved it in her hand, but by the weight of his thin yet muscled body smashing hers she could have sworn it was Richard. It must be fear causing the sweet hallucination. Because that was impossible, since she'd seen with her own eyes how the Czech bastard had slit his throat.

Her soul had died back there in the camp and she'd barely noticed what the mob had done to her, her mind clouded with grief for the man she loved more than life itself.

But now, as a brute dragged her toward the gallows where a noose swung softly in the breeze as if inviting her to go on the swings, her fighting spirit woke anew, and she used to knife in her palm to cut through the rope tied around her wrists.

She had no idea what to do next or how to escape through a crowd of hostile people, but she would fight until her last breath. It wasn't anymore her life alone that stood on the line. She placed a foot on the rickety stairs leading up to the deck, praying for an opportunity to flee.

"Come on, you whore. Get up here and pay for your crimes."

Katrina felt like screaming at the God and the world. This couldn't be possible. Bitter tears slid down her cheeks. What an irony of fate that she'd take her last breath with the safe haven of the American sector in sight.

As she reached the top deck, a shot rang through the air and the guards turned around to see who'd fired it. Katrina, though, didn't waste a single second and dropped her bonds, jumping down from the deck even as one of the Russian soldiers complained, "Turn the bitches around, we want to see their faces when they take their last breath."

In the ensuing tumult, nobody seemed to care about her as she ducked away. Her gaze fell on the shawl of an elderly woman and she ripped it off her shoulders, tying it into a headscarf over her bald patch.

She heard yelling and shouting as the men at the gallows noticed one of the women had gone missing, but she had already half-crawled to the end of the crowd and ran away from the town square as fast as she could.

The wounds on her head throbbing with every step she took, her heart pumping violently against her ribs, she finally reached the woods encircling the small town. Breathing hard, she flopped down against the trunk of a tree, listening to telltale footfalls of people searching for her.

She assumed they'd search for her on the other side of town, trying to escape across the border, so she decided to return to the campsite. Maybe she could at least bury Richard's body and say good-bye to him before she decided what to do next.

CHAPTER 23

R ichard witnessed the commotion, and he very nearly strangled the despicable Russian soldiers with his own hands. Instead of restoring order as they were supposed to they had the nerve to complain that they didn't get a prime view of the gruesome spectacle on stage.

He thought of Friedrich Schiller's play *Mary Stuart, Queen of Scots*, who'd been beheaded, and about Henry VIII's unfortunate wives Anne Boleyn and Catherine Howard, who'd been beheaded as well. It seemed to be a recurring pattern in history that public executions of those considered traitors attracted the masses and made for good entertainment.

A shudder crawled up his neck, but when he returned his eyes to the deck with the gallows, Katrina had vanished. The guards yelled in panic after their prisoner, but she'd slipped into the crowd and disappeared.

He couldn't be sure she'd recognized him when he'd shoved the knife into her hands, because he hadn't dared to even whisper a word for fear the guard would become suspicious.

Trying to find her current hideout was like searching for the proverbial needle in a haystack. What if he never found her again? His heart tightened painfully, and the thought chased away his breath.

It didn't make for a good plan to linger in town and wait. If she had any sense, and she had a lot, she'd run as fast and as far as she could. The question was whether she'd stop to look for him and where.

Hoping she followed the same train of thought, he decided to return to the campsite where they'd spent the night. The nearer he came to it, the slower his steps became, as his heart filled with dread. Only trampled grass and broken things bearing witness to the happenings last night remained. Not a soul in sight.

In the distance he saw the American flag, indicating the demarcation line, but even that sight didn't heighten his spirits. What use was freedom if Katrina wasn't by his side? What if he crossed and could never return to reunite with her?

No, the safe haven had to wait. He'd stay in these hostile lands until he either found her or got captured by the Russians... or killed by the Czechs.

At the place where only hours ago he and Katrina had lain together, confident that the treacherous trip across eastern Europe was about to come to an end, he slumped to the ground and waited.

The sun climbed the sky and burnt down mercilessly on him, but he didn't have the strength to get up and seek out the shadow of the trees further down the road. Instead he stretched out on the earth, his overtaxed brain smelling the lingering scent of Katrina and producing her sweet voice until he dozed off from sheer exhaustion.

Katrina reached the deserted campsite, acutely aware of its emptiness. A haunted silence hung across the place and she couldn't make herself walk any further. Instead she took a turn down to the shore of the lake to wash the blood and dirt from her head and face.

She carefully scrubbed the cuts on her bald head, grateful that the butchering barber hadn't hurt her on purpose. Wandering around, she soon found some chamomile that she rubbed on her head for the disinfecting and healing properties it possessed. Then she tied the stolen shawl into a tidy headscarf and glanced at her reflection in the shallow water. Despite the budding bruise on her cheekbone, she looked like any farmwoman, and not like a shorn, shamed and narrowly escaped collaborator.

With a shudder she thought of the two other women and their fate. She hadn't been able to save them and now guilt settled in her soul. Quickly she scrubbed her hands in the water as if she could wash the unsettling feeling away. After quenching her thirst, she glanced back at the campsite, which lay in silence. Soon more refugees would arrive, hoping and praying to reach the safety of Germany before someone decided to have fun torturing and killing them.

Despite everything the Nazis – and all of the Germans – had done to her country, her people, she still shunned the brutality of revenge; paying for blood with blood would only throw everyone deeper into desperation and chaos.

She would have to leave this place, before another group arrived. Danger loomed and threatened around every corner. What if the Czech bandits returned at night and recognized her? She sighed. Without Richard she had no intention of entering Germany. She'd be better off returning to her farm in Lodz and finding out if any of her brothers had survived the war. As much as she dreaded the several-hundred-mile walk back, she couldn't stay here.

With new determination she got up, rubbed her stomach, smiled, and turned east. At least she'd have something of Richard with her, even though he was dead.

About two hundred yards down the road she heard a groan and she jumped, turning around. She squinted her eyes against the sun, but couldn't see anything. *Probably just the branch of a bush in the wind. I'm getting paranoid. There's nobody following me. They assume I'm German so they won't expect me to head east.*

Another growl cut through the air and she waged an internal war over running or investigating the sound. What if someone needed her help? Finally, she succumbed and walked to the place strewn with the broken things the refugees had left after the vicious attack last night.

Then she saw a body lying flat on the ground and her heart hammered staccato against her ribs. Reluctantly she approached the person until she recognized the tousled blond hair. Tears shot to her eyes, as she pondered the possibility that Richard wasn't dead – yet.

Her feet running as fast as they could, she dropped by his side, holding her breath when she noticed the bandage around his neck. He didn't move, not even when she felt for his pulse. Slow but strong.

"Richard, my darling, my love, you are alive!" She crushed his body with hers, unable to contain the joy and relief.

"Katrina? Sweetheart? Is this really you?" he whispered coarsely at the same time as he opened his eyes. The sound of her name on his lips was the sweetest thing she'd ever heard.

"Yes. Yes. Yes."

He pressed the air from her lungs with his embrace. "Oh, my goodness, I thought I wouldn't ever see you again."

She moaned when he touched the bruises on her back.

"I'm sorry. I needed to hold you to make sure you're not a ghost," he apologized.

"I came close to becoming one today. But someone put a knife..." She cocked her head to scrutinize the familiar face with the beautiful blue eyes. "It was you, wasn't it?"

"Yes." He nodded, holding her gingerly. "You didn't expect me to let you die without trying to save you, did you?"

A single tear slid down her cheek and she whispered, "I... I thought you were dead. That partisan, I saw him cut your throat."

"The cut was only superficial, and one of the women dressed the wound."

"I can see that." She smiled at him. "Did she clean the wound?"

Richard's chuckle turned into a grimace, caused by the pain he must feel when his throat stretched the skin on his neck. "Yes, she did."

Katrina's sanity hung by a thin thread and she needed a distraction to cope with the emotions that threatened to overwhelm her. Reverting to her role as healer, she used her best no-nonsense voice and pretended he was just another wounded soldier. "Did she use chamomile or another medicinal herb to speed up the healing?"

"I have no idea."

"Let me have a look."

"I'm all yours." Richard smiled and moved his head to give her better access.

She knew he was indulging her, because usually he teased her before he even considered letting her look at a scratch he considered nothing serious. Actually, he considered any wound short of a missing limb *not serious*.

A small smile stole its way onto her lips and she felt the tension in her body easing away. With nimble fingers she removed the dressing and scrutinized the wound.

"It looks like the woman has done good work, but I'll cover the cut with chamomile leaves to prevent an infection."

He didn't say a word and only gritted his teeth harder when she dressed the wound again.

"Try not to swallow much for at least a day," she said.

"That won't be difficult, since we ran out of food days ago."

The remark reminded her of her own growling stomach, but they had more important problems to address right now.

His hand found hers and he whispered, "Thank you. What about you?"

"What about me?" With her sorrow over him she had completely forgotten about her own battered condition.

"You must be hurt, too. I saw the barber..." He raised his hand to touch her face where the headscarf ended.

"It's nothing, really," she tried to reassure him, but the expression on his face made it clear he didn't believe a single word. "Alright, it was a real mess, but I cleaned the cuts and put chamomile on them. With the scarf nobody is the wiser as to what happened."

His hand lightly caressed her cheek and a finger tapped on her lips. "I know you're putting on a brave face so I won't worry. But I do worry about you. A lot."

The tenderness in his voice threatened to break the dam of her unshed tears and she quickly shook her head and said, "You can worry later. Now we have to get going. I'm not waiting here like a sitting duck for the Czech bandits to return."

"What do you suggest we do?" he asked.

"Stick to our original plan, of course. Crossing over into the American zone. We leave this very instant." Her entire body hurt with every breath she took, but pain wouldn't deter her from leaving this accursed region and its hateful citizens.

CHAPTER 24

I t took them less than an hour to reach the crossing point into the American sector. Shortly before the checkpoint they witnessed a group of young German soldiers held up and frogmarched over to the Russian officer on duty.

"So it's true. They're sending everyone back," Richard murmured, hot and cold shivers running down his spine. After everything they'd been through, he didn't know if he could withstand another setback. Disguised as a civilian he might not even receive the courtesy of being handed over to the Ivan. The Ami might shoot him on the spot for being a spy. Just like the road signs had warned.

"We need to come up with a plan," Katrina said and pulled him away from the road leading to the border patrol. They settled in the shadows of a destroyed building, and she handed him some leaves to chew on.

He eyed the greens distastefully, but at this point he was too grateful for the tiniest morsel to eat. Teasing her about feeding him rabbit food would have to wait until better times.

"What now?" he asked, observing the queue of refugees lining up at the border control station.

"Pretending to be Polish slave workers won't cut it." She chewed on her leaf, furrowing her brow in deep thinking.

"Right. We need to be Germans, or we wouldn't have a reason to flee into what's left of the Reich," he said with a cynical smirk. Personally, he could have done without the war and stayed with his family in Berlin, completing his high school education with the *Abitur*, and going to study German language and literature at the University of Berlin.

"I can easily pretend to be German," Katrina said. "I don't think the Amis will notice my accent. If they do, we can tell them I was born in Lodz to German parents and have lived there all my life."

"I'm sure that giving the soldier in charge one of your charming smiles will help as well."

"Like this?" She batted her eyelashes at him, and he suddenly felt a deep-rooted jealousy taking hold of him.

Fighting the unwelcome emotion he said, "Maybe that's a bit too much. You don't want him so smitten he steals you away from me."

"Nobody could steal me away from you. I love only you. But you know that, don't you?"

He knew, but it still warmed his heart to hear it coming from her lips.

"I love you, too, Katrina, and I'm planning to marry you as soon as I have proper papers again." He wrapped his arm around her shoulder and she leaned into him.

"Nothing but talk," she giggled. "You've been telling me that for more than a year."

"And it worked, didn't it? You're still by my side, hoping I'll make an honest woman of you one day." He proceeded to kiss her, but after a few short moments, she pushed him away.

"Mister, we need to think."

"About what?" He loved to tease her, and he loved even more the way her brown eyes sparked with delight when she giggled at him. It erased some of the anxiety he felt about the imminent border crossing.

"Well, for one, we need to come up with an explanation why you, a twenty-year-old German male, has never been drafted into the Wehrmacht."

He gulped, the slashing pain reminding him of the cut on his throat. "I could have been wounded?"

"Wounded? No. But sick maybe. Too sick to serve." She scrunched her nose, no doubt digging into the memory of every medicine book she'd ever read.

"My pal Klaus wasn't drafted, because of his severe asthma. He never could play sports with us and at times he'd turn blue in his face from the lack of oxygen."

Katrina nodded. "Yes. That might work. I could give you oleander to make your lips turn blue…"

His eyes widened. "Oleander is poisonous."

"Yes but eating only the tiniest bit of it won't do you serious harm. And it would make your asthma look more real. Unfortunately, I don't think I can find it around here." She made a sad face, and Richard wondered whether she'd actually be willing to poison him to make their ruse more believable. In any case, he was glad that he wouldn't have to find out.

"I'll just cough a bit and pretend to be short-winded."

Katrina shook her head. "I don't know if that will work."

"It has to. I know it's a flimsy story, but it's the best we have. Ready to tackle the bull?" Richard stood up and pulled her to her feet.

Katrina nodded and slipped her arm through his. "As ready as I'm ever going to be."

Trepidation slowed down Katrina's steps as the border checkpoint loomed ahead. Only the hope of reaching safety on the other side propelled her forward – and Richard's calming hand in hers.

"Good day," she said in her best school English to the soldier and bestowed a smile upon him, just like Richard had suggested.

"Good afternoon, miss," the soldier answered, apparently delighted that she spoke his language. "Papers please."

"I'm sorry, Czech partisans attacked us last night and robbed us of everything, including our papers." She had tucked away her identification deep inside her brassiere, thinking it best not to let the Amis know she was a Pole.

"Aha." He raised a brow, the smile disappearing from his face. "What's your name?"

"Katharina Klausen."

"Where are you headed?"

"To Kleindorf near Munich, where the aunt of my

husband lives." She turned to point at Richard, waiting next in line.

The pleasant expression on the soldier's face completely disappeared and he waved Richard forward. "Papers?"

"I don't have any, we were robbed last night."

"I get it. You were robbed. The Czechs stole your papers, but didn't otherwise harm you, right? How many times do you think I have heard this story from German males your age?"

Richard grimaced and pointed to the dressing around his neck. "They almost killed me, cutting my throat."

"They don't take kindly to Wehrmacht deserters posing as civilians," the soldier said.

They don't take kindly to anyone German or believed to help the Germans. "Sir, please, believe us. My husband was never drafted." She cast the man an apologetic smile. "He doesn't like to mention this, but his asthma at times is so bad, he turns blue in the face and he never could participate in any sports." She felt Richard's stare bore into her back, but now wasn't the time for false shame. At least he had the good sense to press out some ragged huffs.

"He looks healthy enough. Tell your lies to the Russians," the GI said.

"Please, you can't be serious. You know what will happen to me, a young German woman, if you send me back?" Katrina didn't have to playact to make her voice sound frightened.

"I'm sure our Russian counterparts will treat you with the respect you deserve."

"My wife was abducted... cough... by the Czech partisans last night... cough... and only by a twist of fate she wasn't hanged at the gallows," Richard said.

At least now a glint of empathy entered the eyes of the soldier and he said, "You can pass, but not him. I'm mighty sure he's a Wehrmacht soldier, and according to our agreement with the Soviet Union he is their prisoner and has to be returned to their territory."

"You go; you'll be safe with my aunt," Richard said, motioning for her to cross the border. But Katrina couldn't imagine doing so without Richard by her side. Without him, there was no reason for her to live in Germany and she couldn't fathom a world where she might never see him again.

She appealed to the GI. "We have walked more than four hundred miles across two countries to be safe from persecution. Please don't send us back."

"Where do you originate?"

"Lodz, Poland," Richard answered, trying his best to look and sound weak.

"You must have been walking for weeks," the American said.

"More like months. We've been on the road so long I can't even remember how it feels to sleep in an actual house," Katrina added. "Please, won't you believe us and let us pass?"

The border patrol looked at Richard and then shook his head, "Sorry, but your case is above my payroll. I'm going to have to take this up the chain of command."

Katrina wasn't sure whether that was a good thing or a bad thing, but she dutifully thanked him with a big smile.

He grumbled something beneath his breath, and

gestured for two more American soldiers to step forward. "Take these two to a holding cell overnight." He turned to Richard and Katrina saying, "We're going to detain both of you for the night and tomorrow we'll see about getting to the truth. You'd better come up with a believable story or my superiors will return you to the Russians."

Richard inclined his head in agreement. "What about my wife?"

"She's free to pass, since we're only on the lookout for Wehrmacht stragglers trying to avoid Russian captivity." Then he motioned for them to follow the two other soldiers, who locked them into a cell.

Despite being imprisoned, Katrina sensed a peace and calm she hadn't felt since they'd fled Mrs. Jaworski's ruined farm. At least in American custody they were protected from the harassment of the Czechs.

CHAPTER 25

Richard pressed his forehead against the cool steel of the bars in the cell. His head whirled with confusing thoughts and emotions. After months on the road they'd finally reached the gateway to Germany. It would be a cruel twist of fate to fail literally at the last step into freedom after having survived for so long.

He groaned, his fists curled around the metal bars, images of his time in the prisoners' camp in Wroclaw coming to his mind. Cold sweat broke out on his back, when he heard steps coming up behind him.

It was Katrina who put a hand on his shoulder and said, "We will be fine. Nothing's going to happen to us in here."

"I'm sorry," he whispered in her ear.

"This is not your fault," she whispered back, putting her arm around his waist. "Come sit with me."

She led him to the bunk bed, where he flopped down to sit on the scratchy blanket, burying his head in his hands. It was all his fault. He should have left her with her relatives in

Wroclaw, instead of dragging her halfway across Europe and exposing her to unknown dangers.

"I should just tell them the truth and let them hand me over to the Russians. You'd be free to go then."

"Richard, no. Please. You can't give up hope. Not now." There was an urgency and desperation in Katrina's voice he hadn't heard before. The situation was terrifying her, and it was his fault.

"That is what I deserve. In for a penny, in for a pound. In fact, I should receive double punishment, for being a Wehrmacht soldier, and a deserter. Why should I expect mercy when my comrades don't get it either?"

"You had a reason to desert. You didn't want to participate in closing the Ghetto in Lodz and sending tens of thousands of Jews to their sure deaths."

"It doesn't matter. I didn't even try to free them. I should be punished." He slumped against the concrete wall, bitter tears of guilt forming in his eyes, before he blinked them away and stubbornly said, "I'm not going to lie my way into freedom. I'm done with hiding and deceiving."

"No." Her eyes widened in horror. "You have to stick to our story."

"They don't even believe our story. Why else do you think they put us in here?" He growled his frustration to the cold cement walls.

"What shall I do without you? How would I ever find you again?" Her voice took on a desperate tone. On any other occasion her begging eyes would have broken his heart, unraveled his resolve, but right now his own guilt, shame and desperation trumped her distress.

"You go to Aunt Lydia's place. She'll take you in."

"Richard, please don't talk like that. The only reason I ended up here in the first place is because I want to be with you."

"And you will, in a few months from now, maybe a year." He paused, rubbing a hand across his unkempt beard. "I really think the right thing to do is for me to tell them the truth."

"I'm with child."

Richard opened his mouth to speak and then closed it. "What?" he said, sure he'd heard her wrong. "You are pregnant?"

"Yes. I wasn't going to tell you until we reached your aunt's place..."

"But wh...?" He didn't need to ask why she'd kept the news hidden. He would have gone crazy with sorrow for her and the child. The thought alone of all the hardships they'd endured during their journey sent icy shivers down his spine. Some kind of man he was, letting his pregnant woman walk across enemy lands, without food or shelter.

"Are you sure?" he asked, turning so that he could see her face.

"Very sure. I'm about three months along."

Richard stared at her, the shock about her revelation sinking deeper into his brain. Panic surged in him. This was the absolute worst timing, bringing a child into this chaotic world and to parents who had no home, no possessions, not even a country that wanted them.

"I don't even know what to say," he said.

"Say you'll do everything you can to stay with me. Don't give up."

Richard hugged her close, his mind whirling. She fell

asleep in his arms after a while and he took the time to study her beautiful face. No doubt he loved her with all his heart, but he didn't want to become a father just yet. It wasn't fair to bring a baby into this world where there wasn't enough to eat, they never knew where they were going to sleep each night, and most of the people they encountered wanted to kill either him or Katrina.

He had nothing to offer his future family, no money, no job, not even his name. The poor child would be born out of wedlock with a father who was a wanted man, facing imprisonment for God only knew how long.

Over the course of the night, he thought back to happier times, before the war, and his own family. They'd been happy, his sisters and his parents. They had a home and went to school. As a child he'd played with friends. That was what he wanted for his child. He wanted to be a good provider for Katrina and make sure that his child had what it needed to be healthy and strong

In the wee hours of the morning, he realized the only hope his child had of ever having that idyllic life was if Richard made sure that he and Katrina found his family. With their help, they could start rebuilding their lives, paving a future for their child.

He wouldn't be of any use languishing in a Russian camp. Or dead. As the sun rose and Katrina stirred awake, he resolved to do whatever it took to stay with her. He would not abandon her or his baby.

"I love you both," he said with a smile and pressed his hand on her belly.

~

Katrina slowly came awake, her body aching despite the unfamiliar soft mattress. But when she felt Richard's hand on her stomach, she sighed in relief.

"Good morning." She looked up him with a soft smile.

"Good morning, sweetheart. How are you feeling?"

Katrina shrugged. "Like I'm locked up in a prison cell."

"I'm so sorry…"

"Hush. I was trying to make a joke. I'm fine." She paused and then added, "I'm sorry you had to find out about the baby like this. I wanted to tell you once we were safe at your aunt's place."

"Afraid I'd go nuts?" he asked, his eyes full of love.

"Partly. I knew you'd be worried sick about me. This isn't the best time to have a baby."

"No, it's not. But we'll manage somehow. First, we need to get into the American sector, though."

Katrina looked around at the concrete cell and the metal bars for a door. They were at their absolute lowest, owning nothing more than the clothes they were currently wearing.

She heard a screeching door and footfalls, and moments later a young American soldier, probably Richard's age, stood at the door, handing them breakfast.

"Thank you." She sniffed at the steaming mush that seemed to be some kind of porridge. "I haven't had a hot meal in months."

The young man looked at her with a slightly unbelieving gaze before leaving, but she couldn't care less and emptied the contents of the bowl in record time.

"Oh my, this is like heaven on earth." Richard stuffed the white substance hungrily into his mouth, but after glancing at her empty bowl, he spooned some of his food into hers.

"Aren't you hungry?"

"You need it more. And don't argue with me."

She was too famished to protest and ate the rest of his portion as well, but decided not to succumb the next time. He was a big man and needed more food than she did, even though she was eating for two.

"Why are they feeding their prisoners so well?" she asked after finishing every last morsel.

"Maybe this is how the Americans treat their prisoners?"

"Maybe." She smiled. Having food in her belly certainly made the future look brighter. Even from a concrete prison cell.

Several minutes later the same young GI arrived and said, "Come with me."

Katrina and Richard exited the cell and followed the man to another hallway.

"In here," the young man told Richard and then led Katrina further down the hallway to another room.

Goosebumps appeared on her arms as the anxiety of being separated from Richard took hold of her. She had no experience dealing with the Amis, but if they were anything like the Russians, she'd rather not be alone in a room with one of them.

She scanned the hallway for an exit door to dash through, but at the same moment she found one that presumably led outside, she scoffed at her own stupidity. *Shot on the run, that's what will happen to you.* Instinctively she pressed a hand to her belly and took a deep breath. Whatever waited for her behind the door that the young man held open for her, she'd face it with grace.

It couldn't be worse than the mortal fear she'd felt when

looking up at the noose waiting for her neck. Even now she shivered with the memory.

"Please. What is happening?" she asked.

"A special interrogator will be in to talk to you shortly."

She nodded and walked into the room, taking a seat in the solitary chair at the table. Two additional chairs were in the room but sitting against the opposing wall. She tried not to let her imagination run away with her, but despite her best efforts, the rising fear almost choked her.

After a long wait, an older soldier with black hair and a prominent nose, wearing three rockers on his uniform, entered the room and shut the door. Katrina surged to her feet, but he waved her back down. "Stay seated. I'm Sergeant Raymond."

For a moment she hesitated but decided to stay with the name she'd given yesterday and said, "Katharina Klausen." Then she waited while he pulled a chair over to the table and opened up a file he'd been holding in his hands.

"I've been informed you speak English, Frau Klausen?" he said in surprisingly perfect German, devoid of any accent.

"Yes, sir," she said, folding her hands to hide the slight tremble, not sure what he wanted to hear and which language she should use.

"But I assume your German is better, right?"

Relief flooded her system, before she realized that this could be a trap. Wracking her brain about the best approach she finally answered in German. "Yes, sir. I was born and raised in Lodz by German parents and thus I'm fluent in both Polish and German. I learned English at school." She didn't mention that like most Poles growing up in that area she also had a modest command of Russian and other Slavic languages.

"Good, good. So, I understand you don't have any papers?" Sergeant Raymond scrutinized her with his dark brown eyes that seemed to be able to see right into her hidden thoughts.

"No. We were robbed two nights ago while waiting to cross the border. The bandits took everything, including the little food we had left and our identification." She tried to look distraught, but honest, even as her Polish papers burnt hot holes into the skin of her breasts.

"Where's your home country?"

"Poland," she said without thinking. Only when she saw the glint of satisfaction in his eyes did she notice how she'd tripped up.

"Why do you want to go to the American sector then?"

"Because… as much as I would like to, we couldn't stay there." Her skin crawled at the memory of the things she'd witnessed in Wroclaw. "The Polish are on a brutal rampage against anyone German. We wouldn't have stayed alive a single day if we hadn't left." She looked at the sergeant sitting opposite her. He must know about these things.

"Don't you think you deserve this treatment, after everything Hitler did?"

This time she caught herself before spouting out that her country had been the first victim of Hitler and she definitely didn't deserve any more cruelty after six years of dire oppression.

"Personally, I never hurt anyone, but you are right, the German nation as a whole shares the responsibility."

"So you never were a party member?"

"No." She almost giggled at the notion of a Slavic *Untermensch* being a party member. If only Sergeant Raymond knew the truth... but then he'd send her right back to Poland. The Amis dealt with enough displaced persons; they sent everyone back who wasn't German.

"And like all the Germans you never were a Nazi supporter either and didn't vote for Hitler?"

At least this time she could tell the truth. "I was much too young to vote before the war."

"So where are you headed?" he asked, scribbling notes onto the file in front of him.

"My husband has family near Munich. They have a farm and are always in need of hands."

"Ah," Sergeant Raymond nodded as if he finally understood. "Tell me about your husband. When was he discharged from the Wehrmacht?"

"He... was called two times but both times they deemed him unfit because of his asthma. So he never joined."

The American made a face and jotted a note down in the file. "Asthma. That's a new one. Do you really want to make me believe the army that conscripted fifteen-year-old boys and half-lame ancients wouldn't draft an otherwise healthy man with asthma?"

"Maybe our farm was just too far in the hinterland?" She heard herself speak and noticed how ridiculous she sounded. Sergeant Raymond wouldn't believe a single word she told him.

"Okay, then." He stood up, taking the file with him. "Someone else will be in to see you shortly."

Katrina watched him leave, wondering what the next person would want. As far as interrogations went, this one had been civilized. Not exactly friendly, but not unfriendly either.

Another soldier entered a few minutes later, asking more or less the same questions.

"How did you come to be in Czechoslovakia?"

"We fled from Poland and since the Russians had closed the border at Görlitz indefinitely and there was no way to get to Berlin, we decided to take the longer route through Czechoslovakia to try and find my husband's aunt near Munich." She got tired answering the same questions over and over again and added, "I wish we hadn't."

"Why do you say this?"

"Because then we would still have papers and I wouldn't have to try and convince you that I'm telling the truth."

"Well, you can always go back."

She jerked in her chair, looking at him as if he were the devil incarnate. "Never! Do you really expect me to cross this damned nation again, where everyone we met has wanted to rob, rape, torture or kill us?"

"Come on. I believe you're not even Richard Klausen's wife, but a random woman who's been paid by him to get him across the border with your little ruse. The robbery obviously is an invention, as is the awful treatment you supposedly endured." The man leaned back in his chair, his bright blue eyes blinking with delight.

She knew she shouldn't get furious, but his presumptuous behavior caused a switch to click in her brain and she forgot all about prudence.

"You think I'm making this up? You think Richard cut his own throat? You also think I did this to myself?" she yelled, raising her hand to the scarf on her head and tearing it off, her knees trembling with fury.

Shock entered the gaze of the soldier, but he quickly schooled his expression and said, "So, this part of your story might actually be true." He glanced at his wristwatch and left the room with the words, "Time for lunch. I'll have someone bring you your food."

The young soldier who'd brought them breakfast in the morning poked his head inside and put a plate with two slices of bread, butter and some cheese in front of her, along with a glass of water.

"Thank you." She gave him a grateful smile, but he averted his eyes and fled the room. Only then did she remember that her bald head was exposed and he'd probably glanced away in horror.

She tied the scarf again around her head, hiding the ugly tufts of hair and bloody scratches. Then she settled in her chair, trying not to fret. An hour went by before Sergeant Raymond, the first person who'd questioned her, returned. He asked the same questions as before. Her name. Why she was in Czechoslovakia. Where she was going.

She was tired, and sticking to her story without getting tangled up in her net of lies became more difficult as the day went on.

"Please. Let us cross the border."

"Frau Klausen, if that is your real name, may I give you some advice?" He seemed nice enough and she didn't care what he said or did, if he'd just let her go.

"Yes, please."

"We believe your alleged husband is in fact a member of the SS."

"No he's not—"

Sergeant Raymond held up his hand to interrupt her. "What I'm saying is, that by protecting him, you're only making yourself an accomplice. We don't have any interest in keeping you here and I'll personally see that you receive the proper paperwork to travel freely in the American sector as soon as you tell us the truth about this man... but we will hand you over to the Czechs should you refuse to cooperate with us."

Dizziness attacked her and bile rose in her throat as she considered his words. The sergeant seemed to be a reasonable man, but looking at the determination in his face, she knew he wouldn't budge. He really meant to hand her over to the Czechs. Which he must know would be her certain death. Normally, she wouldn't succumb to blackmail, but it wasn't just her life that hung in the balance now. She had a baby to think about.

"What happens to Richard if I tell you what you want to know?" she asked with a feeble voice.

"That depends. If we can prove he's actually SS, he'll be tried and hanged. If he's a mere foot soldier we'll hand him over to the Russians and he'll be a prisoner of war. But that shouldn't concern you. You have to think about your own life right now."

She sighed. "Mine and that of the baby I'm carrying."

Raymond's brow shot up, but he didn't say a word.

"My real name is Katrina Zdanek and I'm a Pole." She fumbled in her brassiere and produced her papers that she handed her interrogator.

"Continue," he said, giving them only a cursory glance,

apparently not too interested in the nationality of a female refugee.

"Richard is the father of my baby. We're not actually married, because he's a Wehrmacht deserter. I hid him on my farm, provided him with false papers and we hoped to live there happily ever after, once the war was over. But things turned out differently and we had to flee."

"Start from the very beginning," he said, suddenly very interested, when she stopped talking.

So she recounted the entire story from the day she'd found him tied to his comrade, waiting to be hanged, until the moment they'd arrived at the American checkpoint the day before.

Once she'd finished her story, he gazed at her for a long time, before he said, "This story is even more ridiculous than the one you told me before, but I believe it's true. Once I have corroborated the facts, you're free to leave."

"Thank you," she said, feeling like a traitor.

What have I done?

CHAPTER 26

Two American soldiers faced Richard across the table in the small interrogation room. They'd been asking him the same questions for hours on end, alternating between threats and friendly persuasion as they played the age-old game of good cop and bad cop.

He couldn't quite put his finger on it, but they seemed to be looking for something in particular. At least he thought it quite unusual for them to spend such an exorbitant amount of time interrogating a simple suspected Wehrmacht soldier. They could simply have handed him over to the Russians, or let him pass. Why were they making such a fuss?

His body and mind were getting tired and he could barely concentrate on their never-ceasing questions. It had become oppressively hot in the barracks as the sun burnt down on the concrete barracks with the ribbed roof. Richard's tongue stuck to the roof of his mouth and it felt like he was gnawing on sawdust.

"May I have some water please?" he finally asked.

"If it were up to me, you could rot away for eternity, Nazi pig," the younger soldier who'd introduced himself as Private Jones said.

The higher-ranking man, though, Corporal Purvis, ordered, "Get him a glass of water, since we don't want him to die on *our* watch."

Richard gratefully took the offered glass of water and gulped it down, even though he hadn't missed the hidden threat the sergeant had issued. Purvis certainly was the more experienced interrogator and was well-versed in all the tricks of the trade. Even worse, he made it clear that he didn't believe a single word Richard said.

Deciding to take the bull by the horns, Richard leaned back in his chair, locked eyes with the sergeant and asked, "What do you want?"

"The truth."

"I've been telling you the truth." Even to his own ears it sounded like the feeble lie it was.

"Look, I'm at the end of my patience and we have other means to make you talk... Horst Altdorf," Corporal Purvis said, his perceptive eyes never leaving Richard's face.

Richard's heart plummeted into his boots. They didn't actually think he was SS-Oberscharführer Altdorf, or did they?

Of course, they did.

The lengthy interrogation suddenly made sense. He'd never personally met Altdorf, but the man's reputation preceded him. Altdorf was one of the most depraved SS men, only comparable to his mentor, the sadistic devil himself, SS-Oberführer Dirlewanger.

"I'm not Altdorf." Richards voice trembled with fear, but also with anger. How could they even believe he was capable of doing such awful things? He'd witnessed his share of ugly crimes and even years later his stomach heaved at the images his mind conjured up.

"If you aren't Horst Altdorf, then there isn't a reason to go pale in shock like you just did," the corporal said, his mind made up.

"I swear. My name is Richard Klausen and I've never been a member of the SS," Richard stubbornly insisted, although he knew that whatever he said, they wouldn't believe it. He knew what happened to SS men caught by the Allies and he certainly preferred to be sent into Russian captivity than to be tried and hanged – for crimes he hadn't committed.

There was no other way to save himself but to tell them the truth. If they even believed him, after he'd spun his maze of lies for so many hours.

"That's what they all say," Purvis answered. "I haven't come across a single German who was fond of the Nazis since I arrived here. Were the last six years only an outgrowth of a wicked fantasy? A collective nightmare that never existed?"

"Of course not. The Nazis were all too real and the people who supported them, too." Richard paused, rubbing a hand across his beard, making a difficult decision. "If I tell you the truth, will you let Katrina cross the border and get someplace safe? Please?"

Corporal Purvis settled back in his seat, a pleased look upon his face. "I cannot promise such a thing until I hear what you have to say, but we're not after civilian followers."

Richard nodded and then took a steadying breath. "I'm in fact a member of the Wehrmacht—" A knock on the door interrupted him.

"Come in," Purvis said. Moments later a key turned in the lock and the door opened as a uniformed officer stepped inside. Richard recognized him as a sergeant and stood up. He could just as well stop pretending he didn't know about military protocols.

The sergeant ignored Richard and walked straight to Purvis. "How's the interrogation going?"

"Good. He was about to tell us the truth."

"I'll sit with you, if you don't mind?" Purvis bowed his head and motioned for Private Jones to offer his seat to the sergeant.

"The woman talked," the sergeant said and then finally addressed Richard, warning him, "If I were you, I'd make sure to stick to the truth, because when your story doesn't align with hers..." He made a gesture across his throat and bored his cold brown eyes into Richard, before he continued. "You may sit, prisoner."

It was all part of the game, but nonetheless had the intended effect on Richard and his knees weakened. Had Katrina truly talked? And what had she told the man? There was no way to know for sure and he could only pray their versions of the story matched.

He began to talk. "At sixteen I was drafted into the Wehrmacht and sent to the Eastern front..." He recounted the entire story without anyone interrupting him.

"So you were never properly discharged?" Corporal Purvis asked as Richard finished his story. He had taken over the interrogation again, after exchanging a glance with his superior.

Richard had no idea whether this was a good sign or a bad one, but at this stage the only thing he cared about was ensuring free passage for Katrina. They could do with him whatever they wanted after this interrogation, but he'd beg on his knees for her safety if he had to.

"No, sir. After the partisans captured me the Wehrmacht must have believed me dead." He shrugged. "I would have been if it weren't for Katrina. She saved me from hanging on a lamppost and then nursed me back to health."

"Why didn't you return to your unit after you were fit again?"

"Because…" He grimaced as the memories assaulted him. "My unit had been tasked to assist the SS with clearing out the Ghetto in Lodz. I just couldn't return. And I would have endangered Katrina, because neither my people nor hers would have appreciated her efforts to heal me."

Corporal Purvis' eyebrows shot up at the mention of the ghetto, but his superior exchanged a glance with him that silenced him.

"I wonder…" Sergeant Raymond pressed the fingertips of his hands against each other, raising them to touch his chin. Whether he wanted or not, Richard's gaze fixated on the motionless expression of the man who held sway over his fate.

A long silence ensued, making Richard squirm in his seat, before the sergeant finally completed his sentence. "I wonder, why did this young Polish woman save you? That does sound a bit far-fetched to me."

Richard's brain went into overdrive and he feverishly

tried to assess what Katrina had told them. Apparently not the part about how he and she first met. In Baluty.

He swallowed. "We had met before."

"Oh well, *that* does sound interesting," Raymond said, a lazy smile tugging the corners of his lips upwards. "I'd love to hear more."

Richard groaned, but he didn't have much of a choice. "We were out on a mission to retaliate for the explosion of a bridge."

"You mean cold-blooded murder?" Private Jones approached the table and stared at him with the hate of an entire world in his eyes.

Ignoring the private's attack, Richard continued, "The SS joined us and killed every single male in the village, before—"

"Does that village have a name?" Purvis asked.

"Baluty."

The eyes of the two NCOs darkened and they said at the same time. "No joke. You participated in the infamous massacre of Baluty?"

Cold sweat poured down Richard's back, making him shiver in the heat. He'd just dug his own grave. "Well, yes and no. Our commanding officer pulled us out when the killing began. We were just about to leave when I saw Katrina trying to hide in a barn. Unfortunately, one of the SS men had seen her, too and wanted to have some fun. I claimed my rights as the first one to spot her and when I returned, I told them I'd had to shoot her for struggling too hard."

Jones's mouth gaped wide open, while the more senior men didn't show a trace of emotion.

"That explains why she felt compelled to save your life. But it doesn't absolve you from the crimes you committed."

Richard's eyes threatened to fill with tears and he furiously blinked them away. "Now you know why I deserted. Doing so was a crime against my army and my nation and I'm willing to pay the price. Hand me over to the Russians, or court-martial and shoot me, but please, don't punish Katrina for my actions."

"Not so fast, young man," Raymond said and waved at the other two Americans. He got up, walked over to the door, knocked, waited for someone from outside to unlock it, and then the three of them disappeared, leaving a very bewildered Richard behind.

He was as good as dead.

And his final wish as a man destined for the gallows... was to see his beloved Katrina one last time.

CHAPTER 27

The minutes turned into hours as the sun began to dip below the horizon, sending its golden rays through the barred windows of the interrogation room. With every passing minute, Richard grew more nervous.

What could possibly be taking them so long? Wasn't it a standard procedure to return escaped Wehrmacht soldiers to the Russians?

He worried his lower lip, anxious over his destiny. His mind wandered back to Baluty and the man who'd been his superior during that time. Johann Hauser. A good man but filled with a hidden disappointment at life.

Richard had become friendly with him, but had always gotten the impression that Johann carried a dark secret around. Something in his past that haunted him. He wondered what had become of Johann. Had he survived the war? Was he now a Russian POW? Would Richard ever see him again?

It was a worrisome thing to do: thinking of old

comrades, friends, relatives, and guessing at their fate. Even if Katrina reached Aunt Lydia's farm, there was no guarantee that his family still lived there, or that the farm even existed anymore... What would she do then?

The full impact of the cruel situation hit him and he doubled over, barely able to breathe.

"Get up!"

Richard had been so immersed in his sorrows, he hadn't heard the door open and now jumped to his feet. His eyes widened and he stood at attention the moment he recognized the insignia of a colonel on the uniform of the gray-haired man entering the room. In his wake followed Raymond and Purvis, the two NCOs who'd interrogated him before.

"Sit," the colonel ordered, and Richard took his place on the chair, waiting for his next order.

"My name's Colonel Sinclair. I have a proposition for you. We would like your help."

"I'm not sure I understand, sir?"

"We would like you to work for us. Interrogating Germans who come to the border pretending to be civilians. We want you to identify those who are in fact members of the SS so they can be tried for their crimes."

Richard blinked, unsure he'd heard them correctly.

"In return for your assistance, you and the woman will be allowed to enter the American zone. You will both live on-site and won't have to worry about housing, food, or clothing while you're working for us," Colonel Sinclair said. He kept his expression neutral but serious.

"You want me to turn on my own countrymen? What if I can't accept your proposition?"

The slightest trace of a smile seemed to cross the Colonel's face, but that could have been the reflection of the sun.

"In that case, you'll have to convince our Soviet counterparts to make an equally generous offer."

Richard nodded. It seemed to be a fair deal. He helped the Americans to identify war criminals and in exchange they didn't extradite him to the Soviets. They'd even provide for him and Katrina.

He despised the cruelty of the SS men and had many times wished that retribution would come for them. So, why did it feel like committing treason to accept the offer?

"May I consult with my fiancée, sir?"

"You may. Inform Sergeant Raymond about your decision by seven hundred tomorrow morning," Colonel Sinclair said and made to leave.

"Thank you, sir. I appreciate the offer." Richard stood at attention as the Americans left the interrogation room.

Once the door closed behind him, he slumped in his chair, staring at the wall; his mind was jumbled with emotions and thoughts. He could only hope that Katrina would help him put things into perspective and make the correct decision.

"Follow me." The young soldier who'd brought her lunch opened the door and beckoned her forward.

"Where are you taking me?" she asked nervously. It was late already and the guilt at exposing Richard to harm had been nagging at her ever since she'd decided to come clean.

"To see your man. He has something to tell you."

Katrina wrung her hands in despair. Of course, they had informed him about her betrayal. And now he'd tell her to go to hell, repudiate her and their unborn child, screaming that he never wanted to see her again. Fear chocked her, making it impossible to breathe. She should have stayed strong and kept to their cover story.

The young GI halted in front of another door, turned the key in the lock and escorted her inside. When she saw Richard slumped on the chair, his handsome face twisted into a grimace of excruciating pain, her heart stuttered.

She fell to her knees by his side and whispered, "I'm sorry... please believe me..." Tears pooled in her eyes. "I never meant to cause you harm... I did it for our baby."

"Shush. Let me hold you for a moment." He put his arms beneath her armpits and pulled her onto his lap.

She savored his embrace, but when she encountered the rigidity of his tense muscles, terror consumed her. After a long moment, she pushed back so that she could meet his eyes and frowned at the inner struggle reflected in the depths of his. "Please, talk to me."

"I told them everything. I did it for you. I couldn't stand the threat of them sending you back to the Czechs who almost lynched you."

A heavy burden fell from her shoulders. "So you aren't angry with me?"

"With you? How could I ever be angry with you, my love?" He placed a kiss on her nose.

"But why do you look like... they are turning you in?" she whispered, afraid to speak the words out loud.

"The Americans, they made me a proposition."

"What kind of proposition?" she asked, worry tugging at her heart as she saw the agony of his decision written all over his face. "Just tell me. Whatever it is."

"They want me to work for them."

Katrina tugged her lower lip between her teeth. "Doing what?"

"Helping interrogate German soldiers. They want me to identify those who worked for the SS and are trying to escape across the border by pretending to be civilians."

"They want you to interrogate your countrymen?"

"Yes. They are looking for war criminals."

A wave of relief took hold of her. She had been expecting much worse. "That doesn't sound all that bad."

"Truly? I think it sounds horrible. They are asking me to turn on my compatriots."

Katrina cupped his face in her palms. "I know you love your country and you still believe you owe loyalty to the Wehrmacht, to your former comrades, but I also know you hate the SS and all the atrocities they committed."

"I wish it were that easy. Sure, I never condoned what the Nazis did, but I still swore an oath to Hitler and my country."

"Hitler is dead. He abandoned his people and committed suicide when he knew he couldn't win the war," she said with a bitter tone in her voice. She didn't understand Richard's scruples and his misplaced code of honor. "What exactly is wrong with handing over the SS brutes to the punishment they deserve?"

"Nothing... but... I hate to be the instrument of identifying them and... How can I do that knowing I will be signing their death warrants?" He seemed genuinely disturbed.

"Any man who joined the SS knew about the atrocities going on, and effectively signed his death warrant the moment he chose to actively participate in that inhumanity," Katrina said, trying to ease his pain. "You'll be doing the world a favor, not betraying your country or your countrymen. Your *true* countrymen."

"What if I have to interrogate someone I actually knew?" He ran a hand through his hair, leaving it a tousled mess.

"Richard, have you forgotten Baluty? How they massacred, tortured and raped?"

"How could I ever forget that day? I met you amidst the worst experience of my life." His expression lightened the tiniest bit. "But who am I to play God and decide for a man to live or to die? It's hard enough to take a man's life when you're at war, fighting soldier against soldier. But to decide with a wave of my hand that one man should die, while the other will live. I'm not sure I can do that." He bent his head, resting his chin on her shoulder.

"What are the Americans offering in return?" she asked, smoothing her hand up and down his back.

"They allow both of us into the American zone. We are to live at the compound with proper housing, food, clothing... everything we need."

Katrina was quiet for a moment and then asked, "Can you do what they want?"

Richard sighed. "That is the question. I know the members of the SS deserve their just punishment, but..."

Despite a rush of guilt over her own selfishness, she

needed to convince him to accept the Americans' offer. Wasn't that why they'd come here? To escape the Russian sector and live together in peace? Even though deep in her heart she could understand why Richard loathed condemning anyone to sure death, even an SS man, how could he hesitate when the alternative meant sacrificing a safe and happy future together? But telling him to put his – or her – own needs first wouldn't help. Not with him. She had to find a different approach to convince him to do the right thing.

"Look at it this way. You might actually be saving the lives of normal German soldiers. The men like you who were conscripted into the Wehrmacht and never committed war crimes."

"How's that?" He looked up at her, a glint of hope entering his eyes.

"By identifying SS, you're making sure the others aren't accidentally persecuted for crimes they didn't commit."

He rubbed his beard and then slowly nodded. "I hadn't thought of it like that. If I'm doing the interrogating, it will be much easier to identify the SS versus those men who are not."

"Much easier for you to determine that than the Amis. You would actually be saving some men's lives."

"I guess I would. Why didn't I think of it myself?"

"That's why you have me."

The boyish grin she so loved finally appeared on his lips as he said, "Don't be cheeky, Miss Know-It-All." He kissed her and then nodded as if to emphasize his decision. "Yes. I can do it. It will be hard…"

"…but I will be there to help you."

Katrina laid her cheek against his and they sat in silence

for moments that seemed to transcend time and space – each lost in their own thoughts.

After a while, the young soldier who'd brought her into the room poked his head inside. "Ready to go back to your cell?"

"Actually, I've made my decision," Richard said, sliding Katrina off his lap and then standing up with his arm around her shoulders.

"Very good. Let me get Sergeant Raymond for you."

The young GI disappeared and returned shortly thereafter with the sergeant.

"Sir, I'm accepting your very generous offer," Richard said.

"A wise decision. Private Jones will show you your quarters and organize everything you need to get settled. I'll see you in my office tomorrow morning at eight hundred sharp."

"Thank you, sir," Richard said.

Sergeant Raymond turned to Katrina. "Miss Zdanek. I hope you may recuperate from the hardships of your journey. Please don't feel shy about asking Private Jones for anything you should need."

Richard and Katrina were taken to a barracks-style building with small individual rooms. She flopped down on the bed, still not really believing what had happened.

"We're in the American sector! We have arrived." She slipped off her shoes and curled up on the bed, exhausted from the continuous interrogations.

"Yes, we are. But we aren't free to leave," Richard said, as he settled by her side.

Several minutes later someone knocked on the door and

Private Jones entered, bringing them clean clothes, towels and a bar of soap.

"Here are your ID cards that you have to carry at all times when you're inside the compound." He glanced shyly at Katrina and said, "I'm afraid we don't have sanitary facilities for women, but I can arrange a time slot for you to use the facilities and post a guard at the entrance.

"Thank you." A flush rose to her cheeks at the thought of soldiers standing guard while she took a shower. Living as the only woman in a garrison of men who had been amongst themselves for months, or even years, would prove challenging.

Richard picked up on her embarrassment and squeezed her hand, before he said, "We appreciate your generosity."

"I'll be back in fifteen minutes to show you to the mess."

When they entered the mess tent, Katrina couldn't believe her eyes. She hadn't seen that quantity of food in years. And for the first time in months, she ate until her stomach told her to stop.

"You'll see, everything will be just fine," Richard whispered into her ear as they returned to their quarters.

CHAPTER 28

A fter getting a good night's sleep for the first time in...
so long he couldn't remember when, and eating a
breakfast that didn't include wild plants or dirty water,
Richard kissed Katrina good-bye for the day and made his
way to Sergeant Raymond's office.

During his briefing he soon found out that Raymond
was a strict but just man. Still, Richard found his current
situation peculiar. For six years he had been drilled to
consider the Allies the enemy, had fought against the
Russians at the front and had killed his share of soldiers
from the other side.

And now he was supposed to work with the former
enemy, turning in his own compatriots. Notwithstanding
the atrocities committed by the SS men, they were still
Germans and handing them over to the Amis felt... simply
wrong. Dishonorable.

The Amis were no fools either and didn't fully trust him.
They had Private Dennis Jones shadow his every step. Over

the course of the next days the two of them became, if not friends, then at least good companions.

"Believe it or not, you are doing the right thing here, Richard," Dennis said, after yet another interrogation.

"My logic says yes, but still… telling on people, on my compatriots, knowing they will be punished, just doesn't feel right, Dennis. In fact, I kind of feel sick to my stomach."

"If you have to puke, do it outside in the bushes or you're cleaning it up," Dennis countered with a grin.

"I'll do my best to remember." Richard nodded as he sat down at the table in the interrogation room, waiting for the next suspected war criminal. Usually he and Dennis would start the interrogation and at some point either Corporal Purvis or Sergeant Raymond would join them. Sometimes they would introduce Richard as the interpreter, not giving away that both American officers spoke passable German themselves.

On his first day, Richard interrogated three men, but thankfully all of them turned out to be mere foot soldiers, who'd been chancing their luck trying to escape into the American sector. He couldn't hold it against them. Rumors about the *Russenschreck* kept every single Wehrmacht soldier in its grip, fearing for the worst.

His heart wept when he told them they'd been remanded into custody of the Soviets as per the agreement between the Allied powers. The hopeless horror in their eyes gutted him and every time it happened, he needed a puke break.

It seemed so unjust. Here he was, safe, well-fed and clean, while he sent others into captivity. But those were the rules of war. The men of the defeated nation had to tolerate captivity until a peace treaty was signed. Richard consoled himself with the fact that it wouldn't be for long.

One afternoon, he entered the interrogation room, where another suspect waited for him. Richard's blood ran cold the instant he saw the man. After several years he might be wrong. But then he shook his head of the clouds of distant memory. He *was* certain.

He knew this man. He'd never forget these smug steel-blue eyes. Had seen him in the garrison in Lodz strutting about in his black SS uniform. Had heard him making cruel jokes about the Jews in the Ghetto.

"What was your role in the Wehrmacht?" Richard asked.

"I don't have an answer for that," the man replied, a blasé expression on his face.

So you think, you're too canny to be caught? "You deny having participated in the closing of the Lodz Ghetto?"

"I don't know what you're talking about. I am just a humble farmer…"

Richard shook his head, acknowledging that Corporal Purvis was intently listening to the exchange, his eyes glued to the expression on the presumed farmer's face.

Richard saw through the man's blatant lies, he just needed to reveal them. He racked his brain trying to remember the man's name.

"Heinz," he suddenly said. "You're Heinz."

The man's eyes twitched nervously, and he stuttered, "I-I'm n-not Heinz Singer. You must confuse me with someone else."

It was all the proof Richard needed. The man had condemned himself.

"I've seen that man before," he told his new employers after Singer had been returned to the holding cell.

"He didn't seem to recognize you, but your allegation certainly disturbed him," Purvis said.

"He's Waffen-SS. His unit was stationed at the garrison in Lodz at the same time I was there. I only saw him once or twice, but I'm sure it's him."

"You actually witnessed him committing heinous crimes?"

"No." Richard shook his head. "Not personally. I only heard what his unit had done, but was never present."

"That will be enough to take him to court-martial." After a glance at Richard's contorted face, Purvis added. "That's it for the day. You can go back to the barracks."

Richard wandered around the garrison, trying to come to terms with his emotions. Black and white didn't exist in this twisted situation, only eternal shades of gray. While he certainly didn't condone the barbaric actions Singer's unit had performed, a cloud of doubt stayed with him. He'd never personally witnessed either Singer or his unit executing these unlawful orders. What if Heinz had been the admonishing voice in the background, intent on tamping down the brutality of his comrades? What if Heinz had been forced into the Waffen-SS by some cruel twist of fate?

The possibility existed, albeit a very small one.

Richard's stomach flipped over again, unable to cope with his inner dissent, until he realized it was almost dark outside and Katrina would be worrying about him. He changed direction and headed for the barracks they now lived in.

He was almost across the yard, when the sound of gunshots rang out over the compound and he froze, swallowing back the bile that threatened to come up. Had the Amis really shot Heinz Singer mere hours after he, Richard, had identified him as being a member of the Waffen-SS?

His knees gave out and he had to lean against the nearest building, dancing black dots blurring his vision. *This man deserved to be punished for his crimes.* But the fact that he'd been the one to turn in the man gutted him and somehow, he'd have to do it all over again tomorrow.

Katrina paced the room, glancing out the window, wondering why Richard hadn't returned on time. He'd withdrawn from her over the past days and it broke her heart to see how much he struggled with his new role.

Shots rang through the air and she jumped, fearing for the worst. What if… could he possibly have done something stupid and their new benefactors had decided to rid themselves of him?

When she heard the door open, she turned and one glance at his face told her he was at a breaking point. She walked over, wrapped her arms around his waist, and asked, "What happened?"

Richard just held her for the longest time, sobs of deep trouble leaving his throat every minute or so. After a while, he mumbled, "I knew the man. He was in Lodz. Waffen-SS."

It didn't take much for her to piece the facts together. Having had several encounters with SS-men herself, she didn't actually understand why he felt bad about this man getting his just punishment and said, "If he was SS then he definitely deserved what he got."

Richard buried his face against her shoulder. "Logically, I know it, but... I thought once the war ended I could leave all of this behind. The killing of my fellowmen. The memories... Every time I interrogate one of those poor devils, the image of my friend Karl sneaks up on me. How he died, leaning against me... Will this never end? For how long do we humans want to keep on killing each other?"

Katrina felt his tears wetting her shoulder, but she had no words of solace to offer. After a while, he let go of her, wiped his face and said, "Care to go for a walk?"

She hadn't eaten, because she'd anxiously been waiting for him to return from work, but she sensed his need to walk off his scruples and decided food could wait until the morning.

"I'd love to," she said, taking his hand. Richard kept quiet throughout their walk and she knew he was lost in his thoughts. Searching for a positive topic to coax him from his depressions, she said, "I talked to Sergeant Raymond today. He issued a travel permit for me to move freely within the American zone, although he said that I should not leave the garrison by myself. It might not be safe with the endless stream of refugees passing through each day."

"That's good news," he said, wrapping his arm around her shoulders. "What about me?"

"Since you don't have a valid ID, and haven't been properly discharged from the Wehrmacht, it's a bit more difficult, he says. But he promised me he'd issue temporary papers for you, so we can leave the garrison together and go into town. Although he warned me there's really not much to see and do."

"That I believe." As they reached the farthest end of the fenced compound, he turned to look at her. She could see the tension lifting from his face. Meanwhile darkness had completely settled over the garrison and only a few dim lights from the border checkpoint shone across to them.

"There are so many stars out tonight," she said, leaning into him.

"We've been sleeping out in the open for months and didn't once notice the beauty of a star-filled sky."

"No. We were too busy worrying," she murmured. "But those days are over. We have a roof above our heads, enough food, and you even get paid for your work."

"You know, I'm on to what you're doing here. Trying to distract me," Richard said, his eyes gazing at her in that special way that still made her insides turn to mush.

"You caught me."

"There are better ways to distract a man," he murmured, tipping her head up and placing his lips over hers. He kissed her until she had to come up for air.

"Wow. I think I like your way much better," she smiled, feeling the warmth of love spreading into every last one of her cells.

"Oh really? Then let's try it again with a little more… effort."

He leaned her back against his arm slightly and kissed her. Deep, drugging kisses that stole her breath, thought and sanity. Everything faded away until there was nothing left but them and the unbreakable power of their love.

CHAPTER 29

The Americans treated them well, and after more than a month at the compound, both Richard and Katrina almost felt at home. Life settled into a pseudo-rhythm punctuated by the departure and arrival of a never-ending stream of expellees. Richard figured out a way to deal with the guilt he felt over his part in the identification of former SS members. In fact, after one particular incident, he returned to Katrina, and instead of being upset and riddled with guilt, he felt vindicated.

"What happened?" she asked as he barged into the room with a positive energy he hadn't felt in quite a while.

"I guess I'm finally seeing the usefulness of my work."

"Well now, you've got me hooked," she said with a cheeky grin. "Spill it."

"There was this man today. He'd tried to hide beneath civilian clothes and when asked he pretended to be a simple soldier in the ranks of the Wehrmacht. But it didn't take many questions to bring the truth to light."

"And he was?"

"SS-Sturmbannführer." Richard remembered that she probably didn't know about the SS ranks and explained, "That's a high-up officer, comparable to a major in the army. Once we confronted him with it, he didn't even deny it. In fact, he started a hateful tirade about the Slavic *Untermenschen* who deserved to be treated like the vermin they were."

Katrina gasped. "You've got to be kidding?"

Richard shook his head. "He even went as far as acting shocked that he should be punished for annihilating the vermin. Had the guts to ask the colonel if they had pest exterminators in America and if they punished the men working for pest-control companies. I had to restrain myself from standing up and punching his arrogant smile from his face."

"I'm proud you didn't punch him," Katrina said, smiling at him.

"Believe me, it was hard enough. The vile things he said were enough to make even Dennis, whose German is abysmal, feel ill. I could see him balling his fists under the table and he would have punched that bastard to death if his superiors hadn't been sitting in the same room. Today, I am finally convinced that I'm doing a good thing. That asshole is a good example of why everyone hates us Germans." With the force of his story, he'd talked himself into a rage, still reeling from the impact of how a sufficiently intelligent human being could be so blinded by hate.

"Shall we take a walk before dinnertime?" she asked him, but Richard had different things on his mind, and crept his hands beneath her blouse.

"I'd rather have you distract me in a more pleasurable way."

~

The next day Richard returned to his work with a much lighter heart. His days continued in the same rhythm until one day Dennis said, "Pretty good work you're doing here."

"Thanks, fella."

"By the way, we're pulling out of Czechoslovakia. You should talk to the colonel about what will happen to you and your girl."

"Will do." Richard nodded, dumbfounded. He hadn't heard that rumor and naturally, he worried about their future if his time working for the Amis came to an abrupt end. He returned to the barracks, where Katrina waited for him.

"You look worried, my darling," she greeted him.

Once more he was surprised at her receptiveness to his moods. "The Americans are leaving Czechoslovakia."

"Oh... that's quite the news. What will happen to us?" she asked.

"I don't know. Dennis suggested I go talk to the colonel in the morning."

"That might be a good idea. He might even grant us a travel permit to Berlin." She put on the kerchief to hide the stubble growing on her head, looking positively glowing with the smallest bump forming in her belly.

Richard could only gape at her in awe. Pregnancy seemed to be agreeing with her, as she grew more stunning by the day. He took her hand and kissed the back of it.

"Beautiful." She blushed at his compliment and he kissed her forehead.

"Let's go for dinner. How are you feeling?"

"Fine." Despite the boredom she endured sitting idle in the barracks she never once complained. He admired how well she'd accommodated to living among the soldiers. By now everyone in the garrison knew and respected her and she'd even helped out several times, accompanying a delegation of Americans into town and translating for them.

"I love you, sweetheart." Richard pressed another kiss on her forehead and led her to the mess tent.

In the morning he headed for Colonel Sinclair's office and asked to speak with him.

"Klausen," the colonel greeted him. "What brings you here?"

"Sir, Private Jones told me that the Americans are leaving Czechoslovakia next week."

"You're well informed. Our higher-ups have come to an agreement with the Soviet Union." By the way the colonel's face contorted into a grimace, Richard could tell he wasn't pleased by the new orders.

"I was wondering what was to happen to me and Katrina then?" Richard asked.

"Well…" The colonel scratched his head. "I'm not yet sure what our new marching orders will be and whether we'll still have a need for your services."

"May I ask for a favor?" Richard decided to chance his luck. As much as he appreciated the opportunity the Americans had given him, he still longed to return to his family in Berlin.

"Speak up."

"My fiancée and I would like to travel to Berlin and find my family."

The colonel shook his head. "Berlin? I'm sorry, but that's outside my authority. While the city itself is partly under American control, you need to cross the Russian sector to reach it. And there's no way for me to issue proper traveling documents for you at this point in time."

Colonel Sinclair must have seen the defeated look on Richard's face, because he added, "For what it's worth, I can make inquiries on your behalf, but let me warn you that our relations with the Russians aren't the best."

"Much appreciated, but that won't be necessary," Richard said and thought for a moment. "I have an aunt living near Munich. Would it be possible to go there?"

"Munich?" the colonel asked, walking over to a huge map hanging on the wall.

"Yes, sir." Richard joined him and pointed to a spot about seventy miles southwest of the Bavarian capital. "Right here, in Kleindorf."

Colonel Sinclair studied the map before he answered. "That shouldn't be a problem, since you wouldn't leave the American zone. As soon as our work is finished here, I'll issue temporary papers for you and get you on a train to Munich."

"Thank you, sir."

The colonel gazed at him for a few moments with a thoughtful expression on his face. "I never thought I'd say this, because I was intent on hating all Germans, but you're really a good fellow. Return tomorrow for your papers."

"Yes, sir." Richard wanted to scream with delight. After

their arduous journey, he and Katrina would finally be on their way to Aunt Lydia's farm.

CHAPTER 30

A week later

Katrina stepped from the train that had taken them as far as Mindelheim, about six miles from the village Kleindorf.

"What's your aunt's last name?" Katrina asked, wringing her hands. The nearer they got to their destination the more nervous she became.

"Why?" He glanced at her, picking up the small case with their possessions – all of them acquired during their time working for the Americans.

"To address her, of course." A sliver of irritation snaked up her spine at Richard's nonchalant attitude. Why didn't he even consider that a stranger showing up on his aunt's doorstep might cause a problem? "I can't well greet her with 'Aunt Lydia.'"

He stopped and gave her a bewildered look. "I never really thought about that."

"Of course not, you simply assume everyone will welcome me with open arms."

"They will. Don't you worry so much." He pressed a kiss on her nose. "Lydia's last name is Meier. You'll see; she can't do anything but love you."

Katrina considered his words with another jolt of trepidation. The German people had been indoctrinated to hate the Slavs for more than fifteen years. Would his aunt really accept a Polish woman into her family?

"Shouldn't we at least find a pay phone and give her a warning that we are coming?"

Richard laughed out loud and pointed at the railway building lying in rubble. "Suit yourself. The chances of finding a working pay phone are less than slim."

Letting her eyes travel across the devastation she admitted the truth in his words.

"Come on, sweetheart. It'll all be fine. You'll see." He took her hand into his and gently pulled her forward, down the road leading away from the small town of Mindelheim.

Already deep into summer, the sun burned down on them. She stopped and wiped sweat from her forehead, glad for the headscarf she wore to protect her skull from the sun. Her hair had grown back nicely, but it wasn't much longer than Richard's and she hated the way it made her look like a boy.

Something looked odd in the rural landscape, but she couldn't quite point her finger at it. Cocking her head, she gazed at the ripe ears of wheat until it dawned on her. "The harvest hasn't been brought in."

"What do you mean? It's not yet time." Richard frowned.

She laughed at him, because clearly one year living with

her hadn't made a farmer out of him. "In Poland we'd begin harvesting right now, but here we're hundreds of miles further south and these crops look overly ripe." She closed her hand around one of the ears and pulled, the grains staying in her hand. "See?"

Richard reached for some and shoved them into his mouth. "They're still good."

"But only until it rains the next time. If they aren't harvested by then, all the produce will rot in the fields. What a shame." With millions of people suffering from hunger it was akin to a crime not to harvest the fields.

"Not enough hands I guess," Richard said and picked up the journey down the road. They walked in silence for a time until he pulled on her hand, hopping up and down like a small boy with a look of pure joy on his face.

"There is the farm. We have arrived!" He started forward, but she pulled him back.

"What if your aunt doesn't like me? What if she doesn't want me on the farm?" Her voice came across as a feeble whisper.

Richard hugged her close for a moment. "Stop worrying, sweetheart. Aunt Lydia is going to adore you. I promise." He released her, took her hand and continued walking towards the main house. "Let's see if anyone remains home."

Sensing the tension in his voice, Katrina felt ashamed for her own stupid worries and squeezed his hand. "No other way to find out than go and knock on the door."

She held her breath as he knocked on the door, but no one came to greet them. Her heart crumbled as she looked into his defeated face and she scrambled to find words of consolation.

"They… they'll probably be working in the fields. You know, a farmer is never sitting idly at home."

He cast her a gaze full of doubt, but walked around the house into the vegetable garden. Katrina saw the young woman hanging laundry up on the clothesline at the same time as Richard froze and she bumped into him.

"Ursula?" He quietly said her name.

The woman called Ursula looked up. She had the same blonde hair and bright blue eyes as Richard, and must be his oldest sister. Although, Katrina thought, she lived in Berlin with the rest of his family.

After several moments of incredulous amazement Ursula's face lit up with recognition and she dropped the white shirt to the ground. Richard held out his arms and she flew into them.

"Richard! Oh, God. Richard! You're alive!" Tears streamed down Ursula's face as she hugged her brother again and again. "We thought we'd never see you again."

"You look good," he finally said, holding her at arm's length.

Katrina thought that was a lie. The young woman had deep wrinkles etched into her face, evidence of the hardships of war she – like everyone else – had endured. Ursula was so overwhelmed with joy to see her only brother that she still hadn't noticed Katrina.

Katrina felt slightly embarrassed to be privy to such an intimate moment between the siblings that she stepped back and glanced out at the fields, where she could make out several people at work.

"Where's Aunt Lydia?" he asked.

"She's out in the fields with the older children. Oh, I have to go get her…"

"Wait. I want you to meet my fiancée, Katrina Zdanek."

Richard reached for her hand and pulled her forward. "Ursula, this is Katrina. Katrina, my sister, Ursula."

Before Katrina could extend her hand, the cry of a child echoed from the house and Ursula hurried inside.

"Your sister hates me," Katrina whispered to Richard, wishing she could simply run away, but where would she go?

"No, she's just overwhelmed."

Ursula returned a few minutes later with a teary-eyed infant in her arms. "This is my daughter, Eveline."

"Your daughter? How old is she?" Richard bent down to look at the infant.

"Evie is just over a year old." Meanwhile two dirty-faced girls about two and three years old came around the corner of the house and, upon seeing the two strangers, clung to Ursula's skirts.

"Are they yours too?" Richard said with amazement in his voice.

"No," Ursula laughed. "They are Lydia's youngest. Maria and Rosa." Then she said to the older one of the two girls, "Maria, quick go and get your mother and the others. Tell them Richard is here."

The little girl took off for the fields with feet flying.

Ursula gazed at Katrina again with an expression that was difficult to interpret, but she didn't ask the questions that Katrina knew must be burning on her tongue.

∿

"Come inside. Where have you been? How did you get here? You must be hungry. Have you heard from Mutter?" Ursula interlaced her arm with Richard's, leaving Katrina feeling like the proverbial fifth wheel, and showered him with questions, not giving him the time to answer even one of them. "I can't believe you're back," she uttered time and again.

They'd barely settled around the huge kitchen table when a voice cried from the back door of the house. "Richard! Good gracious!"

"Aunt Lydia. It's been such a long time. You can't imagine how happy I am to see you." Richard hugged the older woman, almost chocking on his emotions. She wasn't his mother but seeing her and Ursula filled him with joy. Then he shook hands with each of the six children lined up behind her.

"You have grown a lot, Jörg," he said, barely recognizing his oldest cousin.

"He's thirteen and has done most of the work running the farm," Lydia explained, before her glance fell upon Katrina. "And who's this young lady?"

Richard could feel Katrina tense up and hurried to say, "She's my fiancé, Katrina Zdanek."

Lydia clasped Katrina's hand and then smiled warmly at her. "You must be hungry. Ursula, help me get them some food."

Once everyone was seated with a bowl of steaming soup in front of them, they caught up on each other's struggles during the war. Richard glanced over at Katrina, noting that the hot soup and the chitchat were easing her tension, and she seemed content to listen to the conversation although she never said a word.

"Why aren't the people working in the fields?" Richard asked.

Lydia's face turned into a grimace. "No workers. All the men are dead, away or imprisoned... and since the war is over, we don't even have the foreign workers to help."

"We do what we can, but without diesel oil for the tractor and only the children and some women from town to help, a day's work isn't nearly sufficient." Jörg nodded at his smaller siblings, obviously counting himself as the only adult man on the farm.

"We'll help," Katrina offered, speaking up for the first time.

Lydia shook her head. "No, you just arrived here and must be exhausted from your journey."

"Katrina is right. Her family owns a farm near Lodz and she's well-versed in the ins and outs of farm work. She even taught me," Richard said.

"You?" Aunt Lydia laughed. "The boy who wasn't anywhere to be found whenever there was work to do?"

Richard felt his ears heating with embarrassment. It was true, when his family had spent summer vacation with Aunt Lydia, he'd preferred to hide with a book in his hands in the barn while everyone else helped with the harvest.

To deflect attention from the misdeeds of his youth he said, "Katrina does not only know about farm work, but she works miracles with her knowledge of medicinal herbs as well."

"You do?" Ursula asked, visibly delighted. "There's no

medicine to be found even on the black market and the old doctor died last year."

"My parents were healers and they taught me everything they knew about using plants and herbs to treat many ailments. With the proper equipment I can make ointments, dressings and syrups. Ask Richard," she said with a nervous little laugh. "I fed him with wild plants, berries and mushrooms for most of our escape through Poland and Czechoslovakia."

A pensive expression came over Ursula's face and then she asked, "Why did you even come here, if your family owns a farm in Poland? You're obviously a Pole."

Richard's heart stopped beating for a moment, but the building tension quickly dissolved when Aunt Lydia took the lead.

"Isn't it obvious, Ursula? Richard and Katrina are clearly in love."

Later that night Katrina sat on the bed in the tiny room in the attic Aunt Lydia had assigned them. Richard came to her and slowly started unbuttoning her blouse.

"We made it. Against all odds, we have arrived," he said, taking off her blouse. His lips moved across her bare shoulders, leaving a tingling feeling.

She watched him take off his own shirt and admired his naked chest, although she had to suppress a cringe at the sight of the ugly red scar on his ribs. The scars would forever remain as a reminder of the ordeals they had survived – together.

"Thank you for saving my life," she said, pressing kisses on his torso.

"I should say the same." He grinned at her, stepping out of his trousers and joining her on the bed.

Katrina leaned against him, feeling the warmth of his body and the love he felt for her. A movement in her belly startled her and she kept still until she felt it again. "The baby moved."

"I love both of you so much." Richard's face broke into a bright smile, even as he laid his hand on her stomach.

"Should we have told your family about the baby?"

He shook his head. "Not yet. Let's keep that surprise for another day. Right now, I want to make love to you and then fall asleep with you in my arms."

"Sounds like a good plan," she giggled like an adolescent girl, nervous as if it were her first time. In a way it was. The first time without either one of them having to hide their true identities and looking over their shoulders, scared someone wanted to kill them.

Richard bent his head to trace his lips over her collarbone and below. When she arched against him, he chuckled and moved his lips back up to claim hers. They made love to one another, celebrating being alive, surviving the worst the fighting armies had been able to throw at them, and rejoicing in this new chapter of their lives.

Thank you for taking the time to read BITTER TEARS. If you enjoyed this book and are feeling generous, please leave me a review.

Richard and Katrina have finally reached safety at Aunt Lydia's farm, but not all of the family members have returned yet.

The next book in the series is about Richard's sister Lotte. She's working as a Wehrmachtshelferin under the fake identity of Alexandra Wagner. In SECRETS REVEALED she suffers a shock when her contact person in the Norwegian resistance is captured and interrogated. Will the end of the war save Lotte's life before the Gestapo finds her out and what happens once she's evacuated back to Germany with all other female Wehrmacht employees?

Pre-order Secrets Revealed

https://kummerow.info/book/secrets-revealed

If you haven't read the story where Richard and Katrina fall in love, you can do so here: https://kummerow.info/book/trouble-brewing

AUTHOR'S NOTES

Dear Reader,

Richard has become one of my favorite characters and after writing the first book about him and Katrina, TROUBLE BREWING, I knew I had to give them a real happy end, not just a half-hearted one.

BITTER TEARS, though, was a much tougher book to write, than I had anticipated and at times I wasn't sure they'd make it. But the two of them persevered, like so many millions of real people did in a similar fashion, and you can't image my relief when they finally managed to reunite with his family.

Unfortunately, the end of World War II wasn't the end of human suffering; for some people it was only the beginning. We can't really imagine the sheer amount of people on the move.

According to statistics close to 50 million people mostly in Eastern Europe and Russia were expelled from their homes and transferred to some other place. Vast areas of Eastern Poland were given to Russia and in exchange Poland received lands in its West that had prior belonged to Germany.

An estimated 15 million Germans were expelled between 1945 and 1948. This is a topic that has been hushed up for decades, because, after all, the Germans lost the war and deserved it. This may be true, but I don't believe the individuals deserved the atrocities committed against them. The Czechs, Poles, Hungarians and Yugoslavs hated the Germans with all their heart, and now committed the same crimes the Nazis had done to them.

I have deliberately only scratched the surface of the unutterable cruelties, If you're interested into reading more about the happenings, I recommend one of the books I used for my research: *After the Reich by Giles MacDonogh*. Be prepared, though, as it details across 500 pages in tiny print the unimaginable things people did to each other.

Once the refugees reached Germany they usually weren't received with open arms (unlike our fictional characters Richard and Katrina). A country in shambles, with a population of approximately 55 million and virtually no food or housing had little means to care for another 15 million people.

If there are prejudices against fugitives today, you can only imagine how much worse it was back then. I hope this book may help to spark compassion for every person on the run from violence, persecution, and seeking for a better life. After all, we are all just humans wanting to be safe.

My own great-uncle Helmut originated from Karlsbad, a city that renamed Karlovy Vary and given to Czechoslovakia after the war. He used to tell us this funny anecdote: After he'd just turned eighteen 18 years old in 1944, he was captured by the Americans in France and sent to a POW camp somewhere in France, but under American administration.

They were releasing prisoners as early as 1946, but they wouldn't release him, because they didn't know where to, since his home region no longer belonged to Germany. Only when a fellow prisoner found out that his mother knew my uncle's mother, they managed to discover her whereabouts and he finally was released in 1947. Helmut by the way held his American captors in high esteem, because they treated their prisoners quite well.

Breslau, now called Wroclaw underwent one of the bloodiest sieges in WWII and is considered one of the biggest human tragedies. Gauleiter Karl Hanke refused to allow an evacuation of civilians, until it was much too late and the refugees, especially the children froze to death during their escape in January 1945.

Of course, when the end was inevitable, he himself escaped in an airplane. But at least in his case, Karma stepped in and he allegedly was beaten to death somewhere in Bohemia.

You can find an extensive article about the Siege of Breslau here:

https://www.inyourpocket.com/wroclaw/Festung-Breslau:-The-Siege-of-1945_70304f

Of course I couldn't have written this book without the help of so many special people. Daniela Colleo from stunning-bookcovers.com has indulged me and my crush for the blonde cover model (he's also on the cover of Trouble Brewing) and even found him a perfect Katrina.

Tami Stark, my editor, and Martin O'Hearn my proofreader made this book the best it can be by cleaning up typos, unclear sentences, or anachronistic terms. I couldn't have done without the help of all these wonderful people!

But of course the most important people are you, my reader. Thank you for all the support, your wonderful emails, the encouragement, the odd typo, and the kind words. I love hearing from you!

If you're seeking a group of wonderful people who have an interest in WWII fiction, you are more than welcome to join our Facebook group.

https://www.facebook.com/groups/962085267205417

Again, I want to thank you from the bottom of my heart for taking the time to read my book and if you liked it (or even if you didn't) I would appreciate a sincere review.

Marion Kummerow

ALSO BY MARION KUMMEROW

Love and Resistance in WW2 Germany

Unrelenting

Unyielding

Unwavering

Turning Point (Spin-off)

War Girl Series

Downed over Germany (Prequel)

War Girl Ursula (Book 1)

War Girl Lotte (Book 2)

War Girl Anna (Book 3)

Reluctant Informer (Book 4)

Trouble Brewing (Book 5)

Fatal Encounter (Book 6)

Uncommon Sacrifice (Book 7)

Bitter Tears (Book 8)

Secrets Revealed (Book 9)

Together at Last (Book 10)

Endless Ordeal (Book 11)

Not Without My Sister (Spin-off)

Berlin Fractured

From the Ashes (Book 1)

On the Brink (Book 2)

In the Skies (Book 3)

Historical Romance

Second Chance at First Love

Find all my books here:

http://www.kummerow.info

CONTACT ME

I truly appreciate you taking the time to read (and enjoy) my books. And I'd be thrilled to hear from you!
If you'd like to get in touch with me you can do so via

Twitter:
http://twitter.com/MarionKummerow

Facebook:
http://www.facebook.com/AutorinKummerow

Website
http://www.kummerow.info